Counting off on his fingers, Jace said, "Sex appeal. Charisma. Charm. Sexy smile. Oh, and cocky. I count that as five compliments. Though, I suppose charisma and charm could count as one, but you used both so I say two."

He watched as the pink flush darkened to a scalding red. Embarrassment, temper or both? "I'm curious," Melanie said, "were you always this full of yourself or is this attitude a recent change in your behavior?"

"Hey, you're the one who said I had a sexy smile." Then, knowing he shouldn't but not able to stop himself, he said, "And I did save your job, so perhaps a 'Thank you, Jace' might be in order after all."

She stepped forward another few paces. "I'm a big girl, Jace. I don't need a man swooping in to clean up after me. I don't need a hero." Her gaze fixed on him. If he hadn't been watching her closely, he would've missed the way her chin trembled.

Dear Reader,

I'm a holiday junkie. I will happily admit this to anyone who asks, though those who know me are already very much aware of my addiction to holidays. Valentine's Day just happens to be one of my favorites. How could it not be? It's a day meant to celebrate love. Sometimes, though, love can be sticky, confusing and downright painful.

What happens when a woman's life experiences have taught her that loving a man spells disaster, especially when the man she's falling for seems to embody every trait she's learned to shy away from? What if she has to work with this man on—of all things—a Valentine's Day feature for the newspaper they both work for?

These are the questions that sparked the story you're about to read, *A Match Made by Cupid*. In this book, you'll meet Jace and Melanie, two people who are seemingly polar opposites but still find the attraction between them blinding. While Jace is ready for love, Melanie never wants to tie her heart to a man.

I had such a wonderful time writing this story, and I hope you fall in love with Jace and Melanie just as I did. And of course, happy Valentine's Day!

Tracy Madison

A MATCH
MADE BY CUPID

TRACY MADISON

Harlequin®

SPECIAL EDITION

ISBN-13: 978-0-373-65652-3

A MATCH MADE BY CUPID

Books by Tracy Madison

Harlequin Special Edition

Miracle Under the Mistletoe #2154
A Match Made by Cupid #2170

*The Foster Brothers

Other titles by this author available in ebook format

TRACY MADISON

lives in Northwestern Ohio with her husband, four
children, one bear-size dog, one loving-but-paranoid
pooch and a couple of snobby cats. Her house
is often hectic, noisy and filled to the brim with
laugh-out-loud moments. Many of these incidents
fire up her imagination to create the interesting,
realistic and intrinsically funny characters that live in
her stories. Tracy loves to hear from readers. You can
reach her at tracy@tracymadison.com.

To my mother: for always believing in
and supporting me. I couldn't have asked for
a better woman to guide me through life. Thank you.

Chapter One

Some days start off bad but end up redeeming themselves. Other days simply go from bad to worse. Despite Melanie Prentiss's best efforts to believe in redemption, today promised to be of the latter variety.

The bad-day vibe began when she lit her hair on fire. Well, more of a smolder than an actual flame. All she'd meant to do was heat up her eyeliner pencil so the color would glide on smoothly. She'd been going for the larger-than-life-eyes look, not the she-barely-escaped-a-burning-building-alive look.

Fingering the singed chunk of hair at her right temple, Melanie sighed. That was the moment she should have taken notice and called in sick. But because her mother had raised her to be tenacious, she'd ventured on—only to spill her grande-size caramel macchiato all over her lap on the drive to work. A little mishap that nearly caused her to rear-end the car in front of her. Not to mention the so-not-fun sensation of steaming hot liquid drenching her thighs.

But did she turn her car around and head toward home like any sane person would've done? No. Something she regretted hugely when she entered her office building, rushing because she was already late, and managed to catch her heel on the rubber floor mat in the lobby. She'd flown across said lobby like a bird with an injured wing, landing in a pile of coffee-soaked clothes in front of the bank of elevators. Minus one shoe, naturally.

And now: *this*.

Melanie scowled as she stared at the hastily scrawled message from her boss stuck to her monitor: *Melanie! My office. ASAP!*

Why today? She'd hoped for a longer reprieve before being summoned by Kurt, the editor she worked for at the small newspaper in Portland, Oregon. How likely was it that he wanted to see her about something other than her latest column? Not very, she admitted to herself. Heck, she couldn't even blame him. She'd crossed a line she shouldn't have. *Again.*

Shrugging off her coat, she plopped down in her chair. No, the blame could only rest on her shoulders. Her emotions had gotten the better of her. Mostly because of her mother's latest broken heart. Loretta Prentiss had at least three of them per year, and it was always up to Melanie to help bandage together the pieces. Her mother was intelligent, attractive, the owner of a successful business, and ferociously devoted to finding her "one true love."

Too bad she had terrible taste in men.

Loretta's men, as Melanie called them, all fell in the "too" category: too suave, too handsome and too charismatic. They laughed too hard and too loud, and the far majority of them bleached their teeth a little too much. Basically, they were too good to be true.

At least the latest heartbreaker had waited until after

Christmas to commence with the wreckage. But with Valentine's Day less than two months away, Melanie wished he'd put it off for another seven weeks. That he'd wined and dined Loretta and gifted her with some roses and chocolates before waltzing off into the sunset.

Yeah, that would have been perfect, and so much easier on Loretta *and* Melanie.

Melanie's gaze landed on the note again, and she groaned. Giving advice that stayed on the right side of the line shouldn't be so difficult. And now… Well, there was a better-than-average chance she was about to be fired.

Maybe she'd be lucky and Kurt would assign someone else as the advice columnist and let her focus on her other tasks. It wasn't as if becoming the next Dear Abby was her lifetime goal. In truth, the only reason she'd accepted the position was to get her foot in the door. It had taken her nearly five years after earning her degree to get this job.

She'd considered herself fortunate to receive any offer. Especially with the undeniable fact that newspapers were laying off more people than they were hiring. So yes, she'd jumped at the position, even though her duties were mostly administrative in nature. Other than her column, she spent her time researching information and fact-checking for other staff members.

Swearing under her breath, Melanie grabbed the bright yellow Post-it and crumpled it in her fist. What would she do if Kurt fired her? She had little to no savings—not because she spent money carelessly, but because she didn't earn that large of a paycheck to begin with—and between her car payment and rent, she barely managed to make ends meet.

She could ask her mother for a loan, but that might squeeze her an extra month at most. Her mom's salon was successful, but not successful enough to support both of them for very long. Melanie tossed the balled-up note into the trash, leaned back in her chair, and closed her eyes in an attempt to ignore her building panic. In all likelihood, she was screwed.

"Out partying too late last night, Mel?"

The rich, melodic voice eased into her like sunshine on a cool day. The fact that such a voice came from such a man only served to irritate her more. Without opening her eyes, she said, "Not hardly. That's your game, Jace."

"That's where you have me wrong. I don't play games."

She cracked one eye open and immediately wished she hadn't. She'd never before come across a man who got to her the way Jace Foster did. Broad shoulders, narrow waist, tight hips, long legs, chiseled cheekbones and dark-chocolate eyes that promised long, sultry nights filled with tantalizing sex. She'd wanted him—no, she corrected herself, she'd *yearned* for him—from the moment they met. But dipping her toe into the water of the office's resident playboy was a mistake she refused to make. Tenacity wasn't the only lesson she'd learned from her mother, and Jace definitely fell in the "too" category.

"Go away," she said, closing her eye again. "I'm thinking."

"Go ahead and think, darlin'. I'm happy to wait…and watch."

Melanie felt him approach, heard him slide himself up on her desk, but she ignored him. Well, she tried to. She did okay until she heard the rat-a-tat-tat of a pencil tapping. Damn it!

"I know you don't see women thinking very often, so while I understand the appeal, I'd prefer to be left alone," she said.

He laughed, a deep rolling sound that unhinged something tight inside of her. And how frustrating was that? "I'm supposed to tell you that Kurt wants to see you posthaste," Jace drawled. "Did you do something to irritate the head honcho?"

Her eyes snapped open. "Since when did you become Kurt's assistant? Are you bringing him his coffee now, too?"

"Just passing the message along, like he asked." Glints of humor, and something else, shone brightly in Jace's eyes. As if he had a secret. He knew something, and he couldn't wait for her to find out what that something was. She was sure of it.

"Spill it. What's going on?"

Jace tucked the pencil behind one ear, his longish black hair covering most of it. Holding both hands in front of him, as if giving up the fight, he said, "Go talk to the boss. We'll talk when you're done."

Standing, she planted her hands on either side of Jace and leaned in close. The spicy scent of his cologne began a curl of heat deep in her belly. "What's going on?" she repeated.

"I said—" his head tilted forward "—go talk to the boss first." He brought one hand up, his fingers touching her temple, and the heat of it forced a tremble that began at her toes.

"Wh-what are you doing?" she stammered. A series of shivers stole over her, and for a breath-stealing second, she thought he was going to kiss her. *Here.* In the middle of the workplace. And why in Heaven's name was that idea so appealing?

Full lips turned upward at the corners in a smile that had surely charmed dozens, if not hundreds, of women before her. His fingers brushed back until they tugged gently at her hair. "I'm wondering when singed hair became the newest fashion statement, Mello Yello."

In an instant, the desire she'd began to feel evaporated. Pushing herself away, she centered herself by crossing her arms. "Bad morning. Is it about to get worse?"

"Depends on your definition of worse."

She angled her head toward Kurt's office. "What do you know that you're not telling me?"

Jace blinked long, sooty lashes in feigned innocence before

shoving himself off her desk. "I'll be waiting for you," he said over his shoulder as he sauntered away.

Without fully realizing it, she watched him as he walked off, his long-legged gait one of lazy sexuality. How many women had been lulled into his bed by the look of those legs in tightly fitted denim? By the crazy, heart-pumping want of unbuttoning his jeans and stripping them off of him, one leg at a time? Far too many, she was sure. And all of them had likely believed in happily-ever-afters and all too easily had visualized Jace as their knight in shining armor. Well, not her. She would *never* become a notch on Jace Foster's belt.

Battling the annoyance rising up, she inhaled a mouthful of air. The sound of a throat clearing caught her off guard.

"You want to have this discussion out here, or shall we go to my office?" asked Kurt, now standing in front of her desk. "Either works for me, but you might appreciate some privacy for this conversation."

Yep. She was going to be fired. "Your office. I was just on my way," Melanie replied, nervous all over again. "Just let me grab my notebook—"

"Don't need it." He turned on his heel with the confidence of a man in charge, knowing she'd fall in behind. Not that Kurt Winslow was a bad guy, because he wasn't. But he was most certainly the boss, and the people who worked for him respected and feared him in equal measures.

Well, except for Jace. He respected Kurt well enough but seemed to fear nothing.

She waited two beats before following, trepidation existing in every step. She'd learned within her first week of employment that the best way to deal with Kurt was to stand behind her work. He didn't like simpering. He despised wishy-washiness. She took a careful step into his office and sent a silent prayer upward that this would be quick and relatively painless.

Kurt glowered at her from behind his desk. His too-small-for-his-face blue eyes narrowed when he saw her hovering. "Close the door behind you."

"Can we do this later? I have to—"

"Now, Melanie. You've gone too far this time."

With a sigh, she stepped farther into his office and shut the door. "I'm almost done with next week's column," she said, hoping if she started with the positive, she could derail the negative. The advice column was due each Friday, to appear in the following Tuesday's edition of the *Gazette*. Of course, she knew her boss was ticked about *today's* edition, not next week's.

"Can't wait to see it," he said with more than a note of sarcasm. "But, Mel—"

"I know why you're mad," she interrupted. "If you'll just let me explain."

"What's there to explain? You're supposed to be giving good advice. If you can't, then you tell them to get advice from a professional. Stating that love doesn't exist, and women who believe in love are deluding themselves, is not the type of advice we hired you to give."

"I didn't say love doesn't exist! Not exactly, anyway."

Kurt grabbed the newspaper sitting to his right. Leafing it open to the correct page, he read, "I've been with my fiancé for over six years. He keeps stalling on setting a date for our wedding but says he still wants to get married. I'm getting tired of waiting around. What can I do to get him to set a date once and for all? From, Never a Bride."

"I know what it says," Melanie hedged. "You don't need to read it back to me."

Kurt continued as if she hadn't spoken. "Dear Never a Bride, If your fiancé has waited this long and still refuses to set a date, then I'm sorry to tell you, a wedding will never happen. Wake up from your delusions and take a good hard look at your relationship. You're better off becoming a nun than waiting around for this loser to seal the deal. Throw him away like yesterday's trash and go it alone. You'll be happier." Kurt slapped the newspaper on top of an already toppling stack.

"See? Told you I didn't say love doesn't exist. And come on, that man obviously doesn't want to get married." Even to her own ears, the argument sounded weak. "I'm not going to lie!"

Kurt leaned back in his chair and glowered some more. His bushy eyebrows scrunched together, looking very much like a caterpillar had taken residence on his forehead. "Then you tell her to talk to him, you suggest counseling, you express how important communication is."

"Yeah, but—"

"I explained to you what we want from this column. We want sound advice, Melanie. Advice that will perhaps actually help your readers, not make them feel like crap."

"You said to go for humor," Melanie pointed out, trying to grasp on to something.

"Gentle humor. But this—" he swiped at the paper, causing it and two others to fall to the ground "—isn't funny. We're not out for sarcasm or snappy one-liners."

"Well…there are a lot of people who enjoy edgy sarcasm. And that style is certainly valid." She huffed out a breath. "Jace uses it in *his* columns! So, maybe—"

"There is no *maybe* here." Kurt shook his head in frustration. "Your audience isn't Jace's. The majority of *your* readers are women who are looking for relationship advice."

"Okay, but—"

"Melanie! Stop trying to cover the real issue here." He ran his hands over his eyes. "Do you think you're particularly good at this job?" He waited a second, and then, "Because I don't."

She winced. "Ouch, Kurt. Maybe I've made a few mistakes, but—"

"I like you, Mel. You are *capable* of doing a good job."

A tiny amount of optimism fizzled in. "Thank you," she said softly. "I promise—"

"But I've given you a long rope, and you've gone and hung yourself with it. I don't want to babysit you, and I shouldn't have to. I need to be able to trust you."

"I get that."

"I told you last time I was going to fire you if this happened again."

She mentally added the twenty-two dollars in her wallet with the less than one hundred in her bank account and somehow managed not to groan. "But…um…you're not going to, right?"

The resounding silence was deafening. After what seemed an eternity, Kurt did sort of a half shrug. "That's up to you. I'm willing to give you one more chance. But that chance comes with stipulations."

"I can do stipulations! What are they?"

He gave her a hard stare. "From now on, *everything* you write is to be reviewed by someone else. If that someone says you change it, you change it. No questions asked. Got it?"

"Whatever you want," she blurted, happy to still be employed. But then a sudden whisper of intuition made her stomach cramp. He wouldn't—couldn't—do that to her, could he? "Well, wait a minute. Who is the 'someone else' you're referring to?"

"Jace."

Shock coursed through her. "Jace Foster? Forget it. I'd rather be fired."

"All righty, then. You're fired. Clean out your desk and get out of here."

Okay. Not a bluff.

Melanie inhaled a breath, counted to ten and then pushed it back out. The only way she handled her absurd attraction to Jace was by keeping him at a distance. This new scenario would force them together way too often for her liking. "You're serious? You're really going to fire me unless I let that egotistical playboy babysit me? I promise I won't make this mistake again."

"That's what you said when you instructed one woman to replace the man in her life with a dog for companionship and a vibrator for pleasure." Kurt pounded one fist against the surface of his desk, causing another stack of papers to topple. "No dice, Mel."

She'd forgotten about that one. She still felt it was good advice. "I mean it this time."

"What about when you blithely told a reader that if her husband was staying late at work every night, then he was most certainly cheating, and she should go talk to a good divorce attorney and take him for everything he had?"

"That could have been true! That husband hadn't been home on time in over a year!"

Kurt's mouth straightened into a taut line. "The problem," he said in a monotone voice, "is that you're giving advice based on your issues with love and your distrust of men. It can't continue. Simple as that."

She coughed to cover her surprise at her boss's words. At the truth of them. "I don't distrust *all* men. But come on, Kurt—Jace? Stick me with someone else. *Anyone* else."

"Really, Mel? You think you're in a position to make demands?" Kurt swept his beefy fingers through his curly mop of hair. "Besides which, it isn't all bad. You've been begging me for an assignment, and I have one for you and Jace to work on together. If you decide to stay."

She was all set to argue her case—weak as it was—when

she realized what Kurt had said. "An assignment? As in an actual, honest-to-God, my-name-on-the-byline assignment?"

"I thought that would interest you."

Yeah, well, loathe as she was to admit it, she *was* interested. The *Portland Gazette* was small, but Jace had a wide readership. Wide enough that he'd been offered positions with larger papers. But for whatever reason, he continued to stick it out here. So an assignment with him might give her a platform to build on.

"What's the assignment?" she asked through gritted teeth.

"A Valentine's Day feature." Kurt grinned at her. "You might actually learn something about love that you can apply to the advice column. A win-win situation, if you ask me."

"Are you kidding? You want me to write a fluff piece with Jace?"

"I do, and you get to keep your job to boot. You might not like the terms, but I'd say they're worth considering. Of course, it's your choice." Kurt's chin was set, his gaze firmly planted on hers. He was not going to change his mind.

She *should* be grabbing on to this with both hands. This was a chance to prove herself. She should feel excited. Instead, every part of her tensed with panic. "Why is Jace even willing to do this? Doesn't he have more important things to take up his time?"

"Strangely, working with you was his idea. You owe him a thank-you, because if it wasn't for him, you'd be out of a job."

Jace's idea? She silently counted to ten before freaking out. Maybe Jace had a heart. Maybe she was jumping to all the wrong conclusions regarding his motivation. She gave herself a few seconds to consider that. "How did this conversation take place, Kurt?"

"One word at a time," Kurt said, completely straight-faced. "Other than that, I have no idea what you mean."

"I mean, how did you and Jace happen to discuss the fact that you might be firing me in the first place? Isn't that sort of a breach of confidence?"

Kurt looked at her for so long she began to wonder if he'd even heard her, but then he laughed. Loudly. "Breach of confidence. Nice one, Mel. Nah, all that happened was Jace read your column and knew you'd be up to your eyeballs in hot water. He approached me, I listened and we made the deal I offered you."

"Right. Because he's so friggin' kindhearted." She backed up and braced herself against the closed door. Knowing Jace, this *deal* was more about seducing her than helping her. He'd flirted with her relentlessly almost from the day she was hired, had asked her out repeatedly and hadn't even tried to hide his interest. "Did you ask him what he expects to gain from this?"

"Doesn't concern me what his reasons are. If they concern you, then you should probably ask him."

Oh, she would. Right before she strangled him. The throbbing vein in her neck calmed while she considered how red she'd let his face turn before she allowed him to breathe again. "There is absolutely no backing out of this?"

"Consider him your other half. If you agree, the two of you will be spending large chunks of time together, so you might as well get used to the idea." Kurt tossed her a half smile. "Though he does have some ideas about the feature you might like."

"What? Ten surefire steps on how to entice women into his bed?" she shot back. "And what the hell does Jace know about love? I mean, has he ever been in a relationship that lasted more than three hours?"

"Have you?" Kurt asked, deadpan.

She ignored that and asked, "How am I going to have time for this along with everything else? I have at least twenty hours of work sitting on my desk and the week has barely begun."

"Give everything to Joanne to redistribute," Kurt said, referring to his assistant. "Does that mean you're saying yes, Melanie?"

Well. She really didn't have a choice, did she? "I accept your terms, even if they are lame and unnecessary. God, Kurt…I can't believe you agreed to this."

Kurt laughed, his pudgy cheeks swelling as he did. "Why wouldn't I? For one, I don't have to waste time interviewing candidates to replace you. For two, I trust Jace's instincts." Lifting his shoulders in a slight shrug, Kurt continued, "Somehow, I have an idea that the two of you will make an excellent team. You could learn a lot from Jace."

Melanie nodded, swung around on her heel and escaped. She had a neck to throttle.

Chapter Two

Jace swallowed a large gulp of coffee and propped his legs on his desk, trying to display a relaxed, laissez-faire attitude.

All a front, of course.

Indifferent did not, in any way whatsoever, describe his feelings toward Melanie. Or his current mental state, for that matter. *Flummoxed* was more appropriate, though still not quite right. A word didn't exist that accurately conveyed the maddening mix of confusion, attraction, yearning, irritation, hope, desire and awkwardness that even thinking about Melanie brought to the surface. So *flummoxed* would have to do well enough.

Jace figured the woman in question was set to storm into his office at any minute, likely with smoke pouring out of her ears and flames shooting from her tongue. When she did, he wanted to be ready. And that meant keeping his messy stew of emotions under wraps. Melanie needed to see him as calm. Collected. *Worthwhile.*

Muttering a curse, Jace downed another gulp of his too-weak brew. For sure Melanie was going to be steamed. Not the best way to begin any collaboration, especially one which he hoped to turn into a relationship.

Whoa, he warned himself. *Don't get carried away.* He wasn't prepared to commit himself to the idea of a bonafide relationship with a woman who barely gave him the time of day.

But he wanted the shot. Wanted to see if what he thought was possible actually was. No other woman had ever affected him the way Melanie did. After countless hours of consideration and many sleepless nights, the reason remained a mystery.

Jace, like many men, had a type of woman he normally went for. Melanie wasn't only different from those women, she was a complete aberration. Stubborn instead of easy-going. Prickly and sarcastic instead of sweet and charming. And, more often than not, an utter mess instead of perfectly put-together. From shirts buttoned wrong to mismatched socks to tripping over air, the woman was a walking disaster.

Traits that shouldn't, under any circumstance, have proved appealing. But God help him, he found every one of them endearing. Cute. At times, downright sexy.

Today was an ideal example. Singed hair—he had to wonder how she'd managed that—coffee-stained pants and, he'd noticed with some humor, one eye artfully shaded with cosmetics and the other eye bare. It took all of his willpower to keep from pulling her to him for a kiss.

He *fantasized* about her, for crying out loud. Which would be okay if all of his fantasies surrounded getting her into bed. He was a man, she was a woman. Those types of fantasies made sense, could be expected, even. But mixed in with those delicious imaginings were the mundane. Washing dishes with her, watching TV curled up on the couch together, and the most recent—going to the damn grocery store with her.

And that was only the beginning of the strange, wacko world he'd lived in since first laying eyes on Melanie Prentiss. She drove him crazy. He drove himself crazy thinking about her. And he didn't have a damn clue what to do about it.

Jace went for another swig of coffee, only to find the mug empty. His eyes landed on the door, which he'd purposely left open, and then at his watch. It had easily been twenty minutes...so, where the hell was she?

A cramp hit his calves. He attempted to stretch his legs while retaining his laid-back, not-a-care-in-the-world pose and managed to shove his chair backward. His ass slid forward as if he'd slicked his jeans with butter, and before he could react, his body—and the mug—hit the floor with a combination *crash-bang-thud*.

He winced, more in embarrassment than in pain, and pulled himself up. Fast. And looked toward the door, half expecting to see that Melanie had shown up in the nick of time to witness his tumble. She wasn't there. Partly a relief, partly a worry.

Jace picked up his mug, brushed off his bruised rear, ignored his bruised pride and retook his seat. This time, though, he stretched his legs under the desk. Safer that way.

Aggravated, Jace turned to his laptop and tried to focus on editing his latest article. He had plenty to do until Melanie arrived. Plenty to keep his mind occupied. He read the opening sentence and then glanced at the door. No Mel. He re-read the sentence and continued on to the second before his eyes slid from his monitor, only to see the doorway still vacant.

"Idiot," he muttered.

He rubbed his hands over his face and returned his attention to doing his damn job. His role at the paper was rather varied. Sure, he was given assignments like any other *Gazette* employee, but Jace's main gig was "Bachelor on the Loose," a biweekly column on dating delivered from a single man's point of view. In addition, he did a monthly write-up, "Man About Town," that included Portland and the surrounding area's hotspots, current events and anything else that caught his fancy.

This particular article wasn't any of the former. It wasn't a lighthearted piece. It wasn't an interview with a local politician or a breakdown of the city's economy.

No, the focus of this article was personal. The subject being his nephew, Cody, who'd died in a car accident a little over three years ago. Jace's older brother, Grady—Cody's father—had taken Cody to see Santa a few days before Christmas. On their way home, they were struck by a drunk driver. Cody had been five.

That first year, the loss had made it impossible to even consider writing about the accident, about Cody. Since then, though, the idea had swirled around in Jace's brain until he had no choice but to act. Anger didn't begin to describe how he felt that his sweet, loving, funny nephew had lost his life because someone hadn't thought.

He wanted people to *think*. He wanted to do what he could to make people think.

In his efforts to tackle the project, he spoke with various organizations and compiled a boatload of statistics. He didn't mention Cody at all in the first or second drafts, concentrating instead on laying out the facts in a clear and concise manner. Neither draft made the cut, as they were dry, lackluster and held less emotion than gravel.

He'd set the piece aside for months while his brain and his heart battled it out. Finally, he gave in to his heart and wrote about Cody. That was when the article came alive. So he interviewed other people who'd lost someone they loved because someone else had gotten behind the wheel when they shouldn't have. And that was when Jace came to grips with what the article was really about.

The piece was truly about Cody. It was about the little girl who was the sole survivor when an intoxicated driver going the wrong way on the highway crashed into the minivan carrying her family. It was about the airline pilot who, upon driving home late one night from the airport, died instantaneously when a car filled with college-age partiers hit his vehicle head-on. It was also about the pilot's widow, a woman who had proudly shared memories of her husband when Jace had met with her.

It was about them: the people lost and the people left behind. And damn, he wanted to do it justice. Needed to.

But he couldn't concentrate, so he shut off the laptop. Another day, when his mind was clearer and his heart wasn't smacking against his breastbone like an overactive puppy. When his ability to create wasn't hampered by a woman he couldn't make sense of.

Jace glanced at his watch again and groaned. Where was Melanie? No way should it have taken this long for Kurt to give her the specifics. Panic struck, tightened Jace's chest and closed his throat. Maybe she'd refused the deal. Maybe she was packing up her belongings now and heading out. No. That was ludicrous. Partnering with him had to be preferable to unemployment.

He pushed his chair away from his desk, ready to stalk out of his office to find out, when she stalked in. Relief punched him solidly in the gut, because, yep—she had flames and smoke. Which meant she'd accepted the deal and he had the time he needed to figure things out.

She'd fixed her makeup and changed into jeans and a T-shirt. The building had workout facilities in the lower level, so he assumed that was why she had an extra set of clothes on hand. But he found it interesting that she'd decided to change before coming to see him.

Kicking his legs up on the desk, he winked. "There you are, darlin'. I was wondering what was taking you so long."

"Planning your demise," she said with a flip of her shoulder-length, caramel-colored hair. "But I decided you're not worth going to prison for."

"Mmm-hmm" was his only reply. He couldn't think. Not when he was busy imagining the feel of her hair against his skin. Of having the right to touch it—her—whenever he wanted.

"Instead, I'm going to... What are you staring at?"

"Your hair," he said instantly, without thought. "It's—"

"Burned. Yeah, I know. You're such a jerk." Whipping her hand to her temple, she tousled her hair. And that little movement just about killed him. "Stop staring."

His lips twitched, but he kept the grin from emerging. "How did you manage to burn your hair? I envision you doing acrobatics with a flaming torch or juggling lit candles."

"That is none of your business."

"I bet you'd look hot. With a torch. Doing cartwheels."

The barest glint of humor sparkled in her honey-brown eyes. In a snap, she masked her amusement behind the sharp glare of annoyance. "Do you know what you are, Jace Foster?"

"Your hero?" He stretched his arms, gave a lazy yawn and tucked his hands behind his head. "Thanks aren't necessary. I'm happy to be of service."

She blinked those fabulous eyes in shock...anger? Hell if he knew. Maybe it spoke badly of him to purposely put her off balance, but he loved getting a reaction out of her. Mostly because those were the only times she seemed to notice him.

"Hero?" she said, her voice low and dangerously even.

That surprised him. He'd be a liar if he said it also didn't worry him. "Where in that thickheaded, egotistical skull of yours do you think I'd consider you a hero for butting into my business?"

"That would be my brain, Mel. The frontal lobe, to be specific." He almost winked again, but feared that might be pushing his luck. "In case you are unaware, that is where reasoning takes place…along with a whole bunch of other stuff."

"Well, I'd say your frontal lobe is severely damaged," she snapped. Bright spots of pink colored her cheeks. "You're a conceited, know-it-all, cocky, pushy dog of a man who uses his sex appeal and charisma to get what he wants." She pointed her finger at him and took one long step forward. "And I'm here to tell you that your charm and…and…stupid, sexy smile don't work on me."

"You know," he drawled, going for light and easy. "Somewhere in the middle there were several compliments. I'm flattered you think of me so highly."

"Compliments?" With two taps on her forehead, she said, "Yep. Your frontal lobe is definitely out of whack. Might want to consider scheduling a doctor's appointment before you completely lose touch with reality."

Counting off on his fingers, Jace said, "Sex appeal. Charisma. Charm. Sexy smile. Oh, and cocky. I count that as five compliments. Though I suppose charisma and charm could count as one, but you used both so I say two."

He watched in part humor, part dread as the pink flush darkened to a scalding red. Embarrassment, temper or both? "I'm curious," Melanie said. "Were you always this full of yourself or is this attitude a recent change in your behavior?"

"Hey, you're the one who said I had a sexy smile." Then, knowing he shouldn't, but not able to stop himself, he said, "And I did save your job, so perhaps a 'Thank you, Jace' might be in order after all."

"It was my problem to deal with. Not yours." She stepped forward another few paces. "I don't appreciate that you took it upon yourself to speak with Kurt about me. About *my* job. I'm a big girl, Jace. My mistakes are my mistakes. I don't need a man swooping in to clean up after me." Her gaze fixed on him. If he hadn't been watching her closely, he would've missed the way her chin trembled. "I don't need a hero."

There was hurt there, he realized. The gleam of it trebled in her voice, glittered in her expression. He hadn't expected that. He didn't know how to deal with that. "He was going to fire you, Mel. I wanted to help."

"I don't need a hero," she repeated. Oh, crap. Her eyes had a definite watery glow.

Jace swung his legs off of his desk. It was time to reel this in, before she burst into tears. He couldn't handle when a woman cried. Any woman. If Melanie cried, he was pretty sure he'd give her anything she wanted to make her stop. His car, his house, all of the money in his bank account…his still-beating heart. Whatever it took.

"Look," he said calmly, "this wasn't about playing hero. I was planning on talking to you today about doing that Valentine's Day feature together. And then I read your column."

Melanie angled her arms across her chest. "So you went to Kurt why?"

"Because I knew he'd be ticked." Jace shrugged. "I actually like when you go all crazy-man-hater woman in your column, but Kurt doesn't. We couldn't do the article together if you were fired, so I stepped in."

"I don't hate men. I just don't—"

"Trust them. Yeah, you've made that clear."

"I have never met a man worth trusting." Her eyes rounded, as if she hadn't meant to disclose that information. There was a story there, Jace knew. Come hell or high water, he was going to find out what that story was.

But for now, all he said was "You've met him now."

"That remains to be seen." She huffed out a breath. "You should know I hate this. I accepted the stipulations because being out of work would cause more problems than dealing with you. But I'm not going to date you. I'm not going to sleep with you. I'm not interested in anything but a professional relationship with you. You need to be clear on that going in."

Her voice held steel, but her eyes were still too shiny for Jace's comfort. So he didn't point out that she sounded as if she were trying to convince herself and not him. "Any other rules before we start earning our salaries?"

She slicked her palms down the front of her jeans. "You understand that I'm serious?"

"No dating. No sex. Yep, I understand." Opening his top desk drawer, he pulled out two legal pads. With a nod toward a chair, he said, "Take a seat. We have a lot to talk about."

"And here we go," she murmured and sat down. "I really hate this."

"Working with me is really that bad?" He shoved one of the pads and a pencil across the desk.

"Well, see…that's the thing. I'm not working *with* you. You're in charge. Kurt was quite adamant on that front."

Ah. That was what was bugging her. The frustration bubbling through him eased. "I don't care what Kurt said. We're partners…okay? I'm not going to order you around or ask you to answer my phone or get me coffee. As far as I'm concerned, we're equals."

"Hmm." Her right eyebrow arched. "Except you get to review anything I write, and if you decide something should be changed, I have to change it. Doesn't sound so equal to me."

Overseeing Melanie's work hadn't been Jace's idea, so he had no problem saying "How about this? We'll just *pretend*

I'm supervising your damn column. Just stay away from the man-hating verbiage so Kurt doesn't decide to fire us both."

Genuine astonishment flickered over her face. Good. It was about time he surprised her. "Serious? You'd risk your job to put us on an even playing field?"

Hell, he'd quit his job if that was what it took. "I'm asking you to trust me. This way, I have to trust you, too." Jace held out a hand. "So what do you say? Partners?"

She hesitated for a millisecond, but then nodded and reached over to shake his hand. "Okay, Jace. Partners. But no flirting. No sexual innuendo. All business."

"Right." He captured her hand in his, and they shook. Her hand, soft and warm, fit perfectly into his. A shot of electricity, awareness, sizzled along his skin, sped his pulse and frazzled his brain. He dropped his grip and picked up his pencil before he said something stupid. Hell, touching her made him want to spout off poetry. If he did, she'd probably clock him straight across the jaw.

In an effort to regain his equilibrium, he angled his head to the side and gave her a megawatt grin. "But, just to get this straight, you think my smile is sexy?"

The corners of her lips wiggled in the makings of a smile. She reined it in, gave him a long look and shrugged. "I've seen worse."

And that, he figured, was the best he was going to get from her. For now, anyway.

Melanie glanced at the notes she'd jotted for the past thirty minutes and tried to dredge up even a glimmer of excitement. Unfortunately, that wasn't going to happen. Not only because of the topic of the article, but because of the man she had to deal with. Being around Jace made her jumpy, made her obsess about stupid things like how her hair looked.

She didn't want to think about her hair. She didn't want to

worry if she had coffee breath or if he noticed that she could stand to lose a few pounds. But mostly, she didn't want to fantasize about what it would be like to sleep with him.

Yeah, he'd surprised her with his willingness to put her at ease, and maybe she felt a tiny bit more comfortable with this ridiculous arrangement than she had when she'd stormed into his office. But she didn't trust him. Nor, if she was being honest, did she trust herself.

The only solution was to change the scope of the Valentine's Day article so they wouldn't have to spend countless hours together. But first she had to get him to agree.

"You know, we don't have a lot of time to put this article together." She tapped the eraser end of the pencil against the legal pad. "We might want to consider alternatives. Perhaps go a different route than you've suggested."

Leaning forward, he set his elbows on his desk and his chin in his hands. "You don't like what we've discussed?"

"It isn't that so much as—" She broke off and gave him the brightest smile she could muster. "We have what—six weeks until Valentine's Day? So, five weeks of work. That means interviews, compiling notes, writing the piece and keeping up with our normal responsibilities. If anything goes wrong, we don't have much padding to recover."

He matched her grin with one of his own. Likely just as false. Because he knew as well as she did that five weeks gave them plenty of time. "I'm pretty sure we'll be fine, but I'm curious. What do you have in mind?"

"Why can't we expose Valentine's Day for what it is instead of perpetuating the myth?"

"The myth being…?"

"The monetization of love and romance, naturally. The pervasive need to spend money on meaningless gifts just because the date happens to be February fourteenth."

"Interesting concept. And," he said with a flirtatious wink, "as appealing as the idea of exposing anything with you is, I'm not sure—"

"Seriously, Jace? You can't stop yourself, can you?"

He looked at her blankly, his expression broadcasting that he had no idea what she was talking about. "I'm confused. I can't stop myself from…?"

"What part of 'no sexual innuendo' do you not understand?" Okay, getting upset wasn't going to solve this particular problem. Reasoning, however, might. "Think about what you just said. Is it really so difficult to have a straight-up business conversation with me?"

Comprehension replaced confusion. "Whoa, Mel. It was just a joke."

"Fine. It was a joke. But if you were sitting here with Kurt, and he said what I said, would you have expressed that you'd find *exposing* anything with him appealing? Would you have *joked* that way with him?" She shook her head. "I highly doubt it."

"Okay. Wow." His jaw tensed. "No, I wouldn't have."

"That's what I'm talking about. You say we're partners, so that's what I want. Pretend I'm Kurt if you have to. Call me Kurt if it will help."

"I can't pretend you're a man. But you're one-hundred percent right and I apologize for giving in to the impulse to tease you." He raked his hands through his hair in frustration. "I'm sorry. The last thing I meant to do was upset you."

He sounded so forlorn and, Melanie had to admit, genuinely sorry. A good amount of her annoyance fled. Deciding to let him off the hook—for the good of the article and their partnership, of course—she nodded. "I appreciate the apology. But all this proves is that my earlier statement was correct."

Blinking, he said, "Now you've lost me."

Like before, she tapped her forehead. "Your brain, Jace.

In addition to reasoning, the frontal lobe is responsible for impulse control," she teased, enjoying the moment way more than called for. "Something you're obviously lacking in. I bet you eat whatever you want whenever you want. And if I had to guess, I'd say that you've purchased many a product from late-night infomercials. Tell me, how many ShamWows do you own?"

"Nice bringing that back around." His mouth quirked. "For the record, I've never bought a ShamWow. But I own a Snuggie...or two." He blinked again. "Maybe three. And here's the kicker. I purchased the first one *before* they were available in stores."

She tried to imagine Jace snuggled up in a Snuggie watching something manly on the television—like a football game or an action flick. A gurgle of laughter escaped. "One of Portland's 'sexiest single men' in a Snuggie. A picture of that should go with your columns."

His face contorted into a half scowl, half pout. "A man has a right to stay warm and comfortable in the privacy of his own home. And, I'll have you know, the Snuggie is a genius creation! I can eat popcorn, drink a beer, work on my laptop, or read a book all without getting...um...a chill."

She tried to regain her composure but couldn't. "Jace Foster, the man about town, the man who cycles through women every time the wind changes, drinks beer while in his Snuggie. It's just so at odds with your public persona."

"Yeah, well, what can I say? I'm a man of mystery."

"Hmm. Yes. A man of mystery who owns three Snuggies." She wiped the tears from her cheeks. "I really need to see a photo."

"Not in this century." His scowl became full-fledged. "And I do not 'cycle through women every time the wind changes.'" Pushing an unopened bottle of water toward her, he said, "Feel like calming down so we can get back to work?"

He couldn't really be upset, could he? She hadn't lied. His dating escapades were discussed in some depth twice a month in his freaking column, "Bachelor on the Loose," weren't they? And that was another thing: she *hated* the name of his column. It made her think of wild animals running free in the city, creating havoc wherever they went.

Another bubble of humor crawled up her windpipe as the ridiculous image of a lion wrapped up in a Snuggie appeared in her head. She took a sip of water to combat the urge to laugh. When she was sure she had her laughter under control, she inhaled a deep breath. "I'm sorry if I somehow offended you. But come on, you know it's a little funny."

"Snuggies are nothing to laugh about," he said in mock seriousness. "However, I get your take on it. You see me as the epitome of masculinity, so learning about my soft side disarmed you and made you question everything you *think* you know about me."

"Sure. We'll go with that."

He regarded her silently for a moment. With no warning whatsoever, the air changed and a spark of *something* passed between them. A tingle teased along her skin, shimmied down her spine, and a crop of goose bumps exploded on her arms.

"Um…so…we should probably get back on track." Her voice came out all weak and wobbly and breathy. *Focus,* she told herself. "Work. The article. My ideas."

Jace sort of shook himself, as if waking from a deep sleep. "Absolutely. Back to business. What, exactly, are you proposing we expose in the article?"

She had to reorient herself, remember what they were discussing before the conversation turned a corner. "Valentine's Day is the biggest con job going. It's a gold mine for greeting card companies, chocolate manufacturers, florists and jewelry stores. If we go that route, focus on the monetization of the holiday instead of the lovey-dovey crap, we'll be able to do most of our research from our desks."

"How is that different from any other holiday?" Jace tapped his fingers against the surface of his desk. "They're all a boon for the businesses you mentioned, and then some. Following that mentality, Christmas would be the worst of the lot."

"You're right," she replied instantly. He had a valid argument. Luckily, so did she. "Partially, anyway. Every holiday is highly commercial, but you can't really put Valentine's Day in the same column as Christmas or Mother's Day or Father's Day."

"Still not seeing the difference," Jace said. The deep brown of his eyes darkened to a near black. If she allowed herself, she could drown in those eyes.

"It's simple." She dropped her gaze downward. She couldn't look at him when he was staring at her with such intensity. "Mother's Day is about celebrating mothers. Moms exist. They're fact. Father's Day is about fathers, so the same deal applies." Not that she'd had a reason to celebrate Father's Day for a couple of decades. "Both have a basis of fact. Valentine's Day sticks out like a sore thumb."

Jace let out a long sigh. "Maybe I should've eaten my Wheaties this morning, but I still don't see what you're getting at."

A sarcastic retort sat on the tip of her tongue, but she resisted. "Okay, let me try it this way. Valentine's Day is a holiday based on an intangible emotion. Not a fact."

"Ah, but you're forgetting the fact that Valentine's Day— *St.* Valentine's Day—began as a celebration for a saint, and was—"

"Right. I know the history," Melanie interrupted. "But that isn't why the holiday is celebrated today. At least," she amended, "by the majority of people."

"Fair enough." Jace cleared his throat. Twice. "So, should I take this as your way of saying you don't believe in love? Or in…I don't know…the idea of celebrating love?"

"I love my mother. I have friends I care enough about that you could say I love them. But," she said slowly, "romantic love is a whole different animal. I mean, you don't believe in that type of love, do you?"

"Actually, I'm a card-carrying member," he said in complete seriousness. "I've seen how love can heal, how it can survive incredible odds. And I hope to experience it myself someday."

She stared at him in stunned silence. A minute passed, maybe two. Finally, she said, "Even supposing romantic love *is* real, Valentine's Day is a forced celebration. The media hype is so overwhelming that men and women are suckered into spending money for gifts to *prove their love*. I…guess I think that's ridiculous."

"Wow, Melanie. Some guy must have done quite a number on you."

Her mouth went dry. She took another drink of water, gathered her thoughts and said, "Gushy, feel-good articles about everlasting love are expected at Valentine's Day. Why can't we cater to the readers who prefer to be single and are sick of the happily-ever-after mentality being shoved down their throats everywhere they look?"

"I'm curious," Jace said softly, but with an edge that made her sit up and take notice, "about what happened that soured you on the idea of love. And I'd like his name and address, please."

Her throat closed and her heart picked up speed. The nonsensical urge to walk around the desk, to smooth away the rigid line of Jace's jaw came over her. In an attempt to make light of the matter, to ease the overwhelming tension saturating the air, she joked, "Why? Are you going to show up with a baseball bat and knock him over his head?"

"Nah," he said, holding her gaze with his. "Violence doesn't solve anything. A conversation isn't a bad idea, though. Point out he's an idiot for…doing whatever he did to you."

"Well." A wave of heat, strong and scorching, radiated through her body. This was crazy. They were having a conversation about an imaginary relationship gone bad. "Sorry to say, there's no one to talk to. I've never suffered from broken-heart syndrome."

Disbelief lit Jace's expression, but he didn't press the issue. She counted her lucky stars for that one. "Here's the thing, Mel. We can't really change the article so drastically. Kurt's approval is based on the way I explained it. But feel free to tangle with him if you want."

"Wait a minute. You let me go on and on knowing that nothing I said would make a difference?" Tossing her pencil on the desk, she said, "Why? You could've said that right off and saved me the hassle and us the time."

"That wouldn't have been fair. We're partners. Your viewpoint is important." Damn him for making sense when she wanted to be mad. "Besides, until I heard your thoughts, I had no way of knowing if we could work them in or not. But maybe we can do a short lead-in about the monetization of the holiday, and play that against the rest of it."

So she was stuck working hip to hip with Jace with no means of escape. She didn't want to like him. She didn't want to think about him. God, she was so screwed. "I guess all that's left is to decide how we're going to find the lovey-dovey couples to interview." She rolled her eyes. "Talk about finding a needle in a haystack."

"Love," Jace said with a smug grin, "is everywhere. It certainly will be easier than finding a needle in a haystack."

"No. We'll find couples who *profess* they are in love, but none of them will be honest with us about their relationships." Melanie was getting a headache just thinking about it. "We'll hear how their lives are like a fairy tale, how life without the other would be painful and empty. They will probably be gooey-eyed and hand-holding and all of it will be fake. Bleh."

Jace chuckled. "I can't wait to prove you wrong."

"Won't happen. Impossible."

"You never know. You might walk away a changed woman with a completely different opinion on Valentine's Day and love." He shrugged. "Stranger things have happened."

Her mother's romantic disasters made even the possibility of that nil. "Sorry. What you see is what you get," she said, mimicking Jace's earlier statement. "Accept it, Jace. Otherwise, you'll only end up disappointed."

Leaning back in his chair, Jace gave her a considering look. "Feel like gambling on that, Mel?"

What was he up to now? "What do you mean?"

He squeezed his fingers together. "A little bet between coworkers. I'm willing to gamble that your mindset on love—romantic love, that is—will change at some point during the course of this project. If I'm right…you'll agree to go out on a date. With me."

She almost laughed. There was a greater chance of the weather turning wonky and snow falling in mid-July than there was of her losing her marbles and jumping on the I-will-love-you-forever bandwagon. Especially in a six-week timeframe. "Um. That's not a bet, Jace. Not when there is zero possibility of that happening."

"I'd say you're afraid the possibility does exist. Otherwise, you'd have already agreed."

"If I agree, and I'm not saying I do, what do I get if I win?"

His brow furrowed. "How about you get a romantic evening with me?"

Now, she did laugh. "Nice try, but let's go with 'no' on that one."

"All right," he said easily. "What do you want?"

The answer came to her immediately. "A picture of you in your Snuggie. And if Kurt agrees, the picture runs for a full month alongside your columns." Placing both hands on the desk, she angled her entire body forward. "I choose the pose and the setting of the photograph. I'll promise the shot will be tasteful, but anything else is up to me. What do you say to that?"

The slightest flicker of apprehension sifted over Jace. Truly, she didn't think he'd go for it. After all, he had his playboy image to maintain. She started to pull away, when his hands came down on hers. "I don't like to lose. Be sure you're up for the challenge, Mel, because I won't make it easy on you."

Ha. *This* wasn't a challenge. "Oh, I'm up for it. The question is, are you?"

"I'm not only in, I can't wait to get started." Lifting his hand, he tugged gently on her hair. "In the meantime, I'm going to start planning our date. And I can promise you a night you'll never forget."

"Uh-huh. You do that, Mr. Confident. I'll start thinking up fun and interesting Snuggie poses." Finally, it was her turn to wink. "You are so in trouble."

"Maybe," he agreed, seeming all too pleased with himself. "But then again, maybe I'll win. There is at least a fifty-fifty shot of this going my way. Pretty decent odds."

Just that quick, some of her confidence evaporated. A wary signal bleeped in her brain, reminding her that she had to be very, very careful around Jace Foster. He was a man who made her want what she didn't believe in. And that, she knew, could lead her down a road she'd prefer to avoid. At all costs.

Chapter Three

Hours later, Melanie let herself in at her mother's house and went to start dinner. They'd developed a routine over the years, one that included eating a meal together at least once a week. More often when one of them needed extra support.

Sure, the weight of that "extra support" landed more often on Melanie's shoulders than vice versa. But that didn't matter. They were a team. Had been ever since the day David Prentiss decided that family life didn't agree with him and walked out on his wife and daughter, never to look back. Melanie had been seven. Old enough to have memories of her father but young enough to get used to life without him.

In her mother's seventies-era kitchen, Melanie grabbed a box of dried pasta and a jar of tomato sauce from a cupboard. She'd found her mom in here that morning, she recalled, sobbing over a half-eaten toaster waffle. Loretta had cried for the better part of a year, though after that first morning, she'd attempted to hide her tears from Melanie.

But closed doors, running water and a loud television weren't enough to cover the sounds of grief. Nor did the layers of carefully applied cosmetics mask swollen eyes.

Late one night about eight months into it, Melanie crawled into bed with her mother. She'd wrapped her arms around her, holding her tighter than she ever had before, and they'd cried together. As far as Melanie knew, that was the last time her mother had shed a tear over David Prentiss. She knew for certain it was the last time that she had.

Melanie glanced at the clock. It was Tuesday, which meant Loretta closed shop at six and would be home by six-thirty. After filling a large pot with water, Melanie set it on the stove to boil. She unscrewed the jar of sauce and dumped the contents into a saucepan before preheating the oven for the garlic bread. A few minutes later, she was chopping vegetables for a salad.

She wasn't expected to prepare dinner, but sitting around and waiting for her mother to come home and cook seemed wrong. With the salad ready and in the fridge, the pasta boiling and the sauce simmering, Melanie dropped into a chair to relax. Hopefully, the evening wouldn't be another rehash of her mother's newest failed relationship.

Melanie had lied to Jace earlier when she said she'd never suffered from broken-heart syndrome. Her heart ached every time her mother's did. It killed Melanie to see the pain her mom went through. Maybe, she thought, this would be the last for a while. Maybe she'd be able to convince Mom to take a hiatus from dating.

Lost in thought, she jolted when her cell phone rang. Probably Mom, calling to see if she needed to stop and pick anything up. Without looking at the display, Melanie said, "We're all set unless you want dessert. And dinner should be on the table in like ten minutes, so I hope you're on your way."

The words were barely out of her mouth, when she heard the front door open.

"Dinner, eh? I thought you'd never ask, darlin'." Jace's deep voice emanated through the line. "Sounds great. Where at?"

Ugh. What was *he* calling her about? "Obviously, I thought you were someone else. And you're not invited to dinner. Sorry for getting your hopes up."

Loretta entered the kitchen and smiled in greeting. "Who wants to come to dinner? Is it Tara?" she asked, speaking of Melanie's best friend. "Have her join us!"

Before answering, Melanie gave her a quick once-over, searching for any signs of distress. Her gray-blue eyes were clear, so she hadn't cried on the way home. And, Melanie noted, she'd had her medium-brown hair cut into a wispy sort of bob that suited the fine features of her face. She looked good. Happy, even. Which meant she was well on her way to recovery.

"Hello?" Jace said loudly. "Did you hang up on me, Mello Yello?"

Loretta appraised Melanie with a speculative gleam. "That very masculine-sounding voice can't possibly be Tara. Who's on the phone, dear?"

Uh-oh. Sensing a danger zone rapidly approaching, Melanie covered the phone with one hand. "It's no one. Just a guy I work with." Into the phone, she said, "I haven't hung up on you. Yet. You've got five seconds, Jace. What do you want?"

"That's a leading question, Mel," Jace said in a light, almost teasing tone that caused her heart to skip a beat. "But seeing how I promised to avoid any and all types of sexual innuendo, I'll get right to the point."

"Jace as in Jace Foster? I read his columns all the time," Loretta said from Melanie's left side. "Why does he want to come for dinner? Oh! Are you two dating?"

"No," she said to her mother. To Jace, she said, "Yes, please. Getting right to the point would be—" The sizzling sound of water boiling over stopped her midsentence. "Actually, hold that thought." Slamming the phone down on the table, Melanie raced to the stove and pulled the pot of pasta off the burner.

"Is this Jace Foster?" She heard Mom say behind her. "This is Loretta Prentiss. Melanie's mother? I'm a huge fan of your 'Man About Town' column." She gave a delighted laugh. "Really! I've always read the *Gazette*—even before Melanie started working there."

And there she goes, Melanie thought with a great deal of humor. Mom, she knew, would chatter about anything and everything if given the chance. That was fine. Mom could talk to Jace while Melanie cleaned up the pasta mess and finished getting dinner ready. If she was lucky, he'd beg out of the conversation and Melanie wouldn't have to talk to him until tomorrow.

"You *should* come for dinner, Jace," Loretta all but gushed. "I'll give you the address. Do you have something to write with?"

"Mom! No!" Melanie said loudly. Maybe too loudly. "Give me the phone back."

"Please excuse me for a second, Jace. My daughter is trying to talk with me. Yes, I know she can be quite stubborn." Turning toward Melanie, she said, "What is it? And why didn't you tell me you were involved with someone?"

"Because I'm not. Did he tell you we were? We are *not* dating." She held her hand out palm-side up. "The phone, Mom."

Disappointment gathered in her mother's eyes. "I guess I should've known better, but you can't blame a mother for hoping. And I don't see why he can't join us for dinner."

Melanie lowered her voice in the hopes that Jace wouldn't

hear her. "I spent all day with him. I don't want to spend the evening with him, too. Besides, this is supposed to be time for you and me. Remember?"

Loretta gave her a considering look, but nodded. "I think there's more to it, and you'll explain every bit of it to me later." Pressing the phone back to her ear, she said, "I'm very sorry, Jace. It seems my daughter requires some mother-daughter time tonight. Perhaps we can plan something for the future?"

"Thank you." More relieved than she ought to be, Melanie removed the garlic bread from the oven and turned off the stove burners. Then, ready to discover why Jace had called to begin with, she went to reclaim her phone.

Her mom was pacing the length of the kitchen as she talked. Melanie waved to get her attention. Mom gave her the "one more minute" sign, saying, "Isn't that sweet of you? If that's the case, you'll definitely have dinner with us."

This *couldn't* be happening. "Mom? I thought we agreed—"

"No, no, don't worry about that. We'll keep everything warm until you get here. It isn't a problem at all, especially with you going out of your way and all." Mom shot her a warning glance before rattling off the address. "Okay, Jace. We'll see you soon."

Melanie stared at her mother in disbelief. "What just happened?"

"Don't you look at me that way, Melanie Ann. I didn't have a choice." She walked around Melanie and returned the bread to the oven. "But I'm sorry if you're upset."

"What just happened?" Melanie repeated through gritted teeth as her mother stirred the sauce, turned the burner on again and covered the pan with a lid.

"He's doing you a favor," Loretta said briskly. "The least we can do is offer him dinner for his troubles."

"Uh-huh. I've had enough of Jace Foster's *favors* for today." And somehow, he'd talked her into a ridiculous bet that she wished she'd never agreed to. "What is it this time?"

Pouring the pasta into a large bowl, Loretta said, "He's returning your laptop, which you apparently left in his office today." She let the weight of that sit for a good thirty seconds. "What was I supposed to do? Tell him he could drop it off but not invite him in? And if he's going to visit for a while, we might as well feed him."

Oh, hell. Melanie couldn't fault her mother's logic. Or, for that matter, Jace's actions. Even if she hadn't remembered until now that she *had* forgotten her laptop. "Yay, we'll hold dinner for him. How thrilling," she muttered under her breath.

Leaving the dinner preparations, Loretta came forward and pulled Melanie into a hug. She smelled like the salon. A combination of fruity and floral shampoos, hair sprays and the chemicals from the hair treatments she'd given that day. In other words, she smelled like Mom.

"You seem really upset over this, sweetheart. I don't understand why, but how bad can one little dinner be?" Mom said as they separated. "How about if I plead exhaustion after we eat? That will have him on his way in no time."

The balls of stress that had begun to tighten in Melanie's muscles relaxed. "That would be perfect. Have I told you lately how much I love you?"

"Yesterday, as a matter of fact. But I can never hear it too often. And I love you, too."

Taking three plates and three bowls out of the cupboard, Melanie started to set the table. *Jace. Here. For dinner.* She almost felt as if the entire universe was working to put them in the same room as often as possible. "Please don't take this the wrong way, but I have a professional relationship with

Jace. Could we keep anything too personal out of the dinner conversation?"

"What constitutes as too personal?" Loretta asked with more than a tinge of humor. "Be exact, dear. You know how I am."

"Anything that has to do with Dad, for one thing." Dumb, maybe, but Melanie did not want Jace in on the whole "my father abandoned us and never looked back" story. "Oh, and anything to do with your love life or my dating history."

With a snort, her mom said, "What dating history? The boy I had to bribe you to go to senior prom with? Or the blind dates that Tara convinced you to go on? Or—"

"Right. All of that."

"Because I don't know about anyone else you've dated." Her mom's razor-sharp gaze zeroed in on hers. "I don't even know if you've ever had sex!"

"Mom! Jeez, that's what I'm talking about. Don't you think that's a little too much information between mother and daughter? Even as close as we are?"

"I've never had an issue discussing sex with you," Mom pointed out. "You're the one who shies away from any talk of intimacy."

"Because for most people, intimacy is *private*. But for the record, so we never have to have this discussion again, I've had sex." Melanie grabbed a handful of silverware. "And why are you bringing this up now, moments before my…um… coworker arrives?"

Her mother, naturally, ignored that question and asked a new one. "Well, have you ever had really great sex?"

Melanie gurgled a non-reply and continued setting the table. She was not, under any circumstances, going to answer that question.

"That's a no," Mom said, adding a drinking glass to

each of the place settings. "Oh, sweetie, I'm so sorry. Every woman deserves a few nights filled with great sex."

"It is not a no or a yes," Melanie countered. "More like an 'I don't want to talk about this, so I'm not going to.'"

"How did I raise a daughter so afraid of intimacy?"

And that was another question that Melanie was not going to answer. Ever. "I'm not afraid of intimacy, Mom." She didn't consider herself afraid, anyway. Careful, maybe. And intelligent. There was nothing wrong with either of those traits. "I like my life the way it is. Whether or not I've had great sex has nothing to do with my life. It is a nonissue for me."

"Hmm," Mom murmured. "That, my darling daughter, is how I know you've never had great sex. Because if you had, you wouldn't be so quick to call not having it a nonissue."

It was at times like this that Melanie wished desperately for a sibling. She wasn't picky. Either a brother or a sister would do. All she needed was someone to divert Mom's attention every now and then.

"You know what we should do?" she asked in an effort to change the subject. "We should visit a few animal shelters this weekend and find a lovable dog or cat for you. It must get lonely here sometimes."

"Don't be silly, Melanie. I'm not home enough to properly care for a pet." Leaning over, she plopped a kiss on Melanie's cheek. "And I have you."

"Just think about it, okay?"

"Sure. If you think about getting yourself some great sex." The doorbell rang, announcing Jace's arrival. Mom nodded in the general direction of the front door. "And perhaps you should consider having that great sex with him. He seems like the type of man who knows—"

Melanie grasped her mother's shoulders lightly, interrupting her. "Mom, I need you to stop talking about sex right now. Especially sex with Jace. Okay? Please? I'm begging."

"I knew it! You like him." Her mother smiled and patted her cheek. "Stop worrying, Melanie. I'll behave. We wouldn't want to scare him off, now would we?"

"There is nothing to scare him off from." Melanie turned on her heel and went to let Jace in. Never again, she promised herself, would she ignore a bad-day vibe. The next time a day began with something as foretelling as burning her own hair, she'd jump back into bed and hide until the sun rose again.

Her ill-fated decision not to do so that morning had led her from one fiasco to another, and she had a feeling that the ramifications were going to keep on coming until she put Valentine's Day—and working with Jace—behind her.

But first, she had to get through dinner. And, thanks to her mother, try to have a normal conversation with Jace without thinking about sex. Great sex, at that.

Melanie opened the door, and the earth shook beneath Jace's feet. Metaphorically speaking, of course. He hadn't yet decided if the sensation appealed or scared him witless. Maybe a bit of both, depending on the day.

She wore the same jeans and T-shirt from earlier, but the muddied orange-red stain blobbed beneath her collar was new. Judging by the scents emanating from the house, he put his money on spaghetti sauce. Her shoulders were tense, her mouth firm. Signs that clearly said the lady was not happy to see him.

Oh, well. What else had he expected?

"Your laptop," he said as he handed it over. "You left it on, so I saved your file before shutting it down." Lifting the bakery box he held in his other hand, he offered that to her, as well. "You mentioned no dessert, so I stopped on the way and picked up a pie. Apple."

"Why, Jace Foster, my hero as I live and breathe," she drawled in an excellent Southern belle imitation. "I think I'm in love."

"Gee, Mel, that was the easiest bet I ever won." He stuck his thumbs in his pockets and leaned against the doorjamb. "And all it took was an apple pie. Good thing I already have our date planned. Free this weekend?"

Her tongue darted out to lick her lips. "You're a funny man." Tilting her head to the side, she said, "You might as well come in. My mother is beyond excited to meet you. Apparently, you're the main topic of conversation at the salon she owns."

"I got that impression." He almost mentioned that his mother was just as excited to meet the "mystery woman from work that her son was interested in," but chose not to. That information probably wouldn't go over well. He started to walk forward, but stopped midstride. "Tell your mother I said thank you for her gracious invitation, but I'm going to take off. You don't want me here, and despite what you seem to think, my goal is not to make you uncomfortable. I'd be happy to show Loretta around the paper, though, if she were to happen to come by."

Melanie gave him a long, searching look and sighed. "Okay, that's sweet of you, and I haven't exactly been welcoming. I apologize. It's been a long day, and I'm… Well, let's leave it there." Hefting her laptop under her arm, she continued. "But thank you for bringing this over. I'd have been worried once I remembered. It was a nice gesture."

"I'm a nice guy." Not that she believed that. But he was bound to prove it to her. "So, you have a good night, and we'll get together tomorrow. I'd like to start interviews next week."

"Oh, to hell with it." She glanced over her shoulder, as if to make sure they were alone. "If you want to stay for dinner, I suppose that would be okay. And," she said with a hesitant grin, "you'll save me from endless questioning if you're here."

"Mothers love asking questions. Mine does, anyway. But she's sneaky about it. Half the time, you don't realize you're being grilled until she's sated her curiosity."

Melanie laughed, and his heart sort of popped in his chest. "Mine doesn't bother being sneaky. She puts whatever she wants out there and expects to be answered. I love her for that, though. I tend to be more restrained."

He blinked. "Um, Melanie, I hate to point this out, but you're the least restrained woman I have ever met."

Shock and uneasiness washed out her complexion. "I... guess it depends on the topic. And maybe the medium." She shrugged, as if doing so would dismiss the subject as meaningless. Jace wasn't fooled. Melanie saw herself in a far different way than he saw her. He wanted to know why. "You should come in before I change my mind."

Curiosity raged, but he set it aside. "You're sure?"

"No. But come in anyway."

He followed her in and glanced at his surroundings. The ranch-style house was small, so the front door led directly into the rectangular-shaped living room. Straight ahead, he guessed, was the kitchen, with the bedrooms and bathroom down the hall to the right. A simple home, but one that looked lived-in and comfortable.

The room they stood in held a long, country-blue-patterned sofa against the back wall, with a matching love seat on one side and two overstuffed chairs on the other. By the variety of plants scattered throughout, he'd say Melanie's mother had a green thumb. Framed photos were clustered on the sill of the bay window, on the end tables, and a few hung on the walls.

"Did you grow up here?" he asked Melanie, giving in to his need to know more about her. "Or are you a Portland transplant?"

"Not a transplant. I've lived here all my life. Well, I have my own place now, but you know what I mean." Walking into the kitchen, she deposited the laptop and the bakery box on the counter. "So," she said from the kitchen doorway, a tiny frown marring her expression. "I'd say let's eat, but I'm not sure where my mom went. I'm warning you, the pasta has been done for a while. It might not be all that appetizing by the time we get to it."

"With enough sauce, anything is edible."

"True enough. I should go check on her, see if she's okay. Do you mind?"

"Of course not," Jace assured her. Striding toward the sofa, he picked up a magazine from the coffee table. "I'll look through this while I wait. Take your time."

The worry lines in her forehead melted into tickled amusement. "Okay, Jace. You enjoy that copy of *Cosmo* while I track down my mother."

He started to reply but stopped when a woman with the most dazzling smile he'd ever seen floated into the room. Even if he wasn't in her house, he'd recognize her as Melanie's mother. They had the same shape to their eyes, their mouths. Even the way they held their bodies was reminiscent of each other, though Loretta had a solid two inches of height on her daughter—even taking her high heels into consideration—and her hair was a full shade darker.

"Mom, what's going on?" Melanie asked in a worry-laden tone. "You're wearing a dress. We never…um…dress for dinner." She shot Jace an apologetic look.

Loretta, ignoring her daughter, rushed over to Jace. Without an ounce of self-consciousness, she studied his face with complete and utter thoroughness. Strangely, he didn't find it disconcerting in the least.

"I knew you were a handsome devil, but your photo in the paper doesn't do you justice." Reaching into her purse, she pulled out a business card and pressed it into his hand. "One of my customers is a photographer. Call her and get a new publicity photo taken. But first—"

"Ah…okay. Thanks." Jace tucked the card into his pocket.

Squinting her eyes in continued appraisal, she gripped his jaw lightly. "Turn to the side, so I can see your haircut better."

Not about to argue, he turned to the side. While Loretta fluffed and fluttered with his hair, he winked at Melanie. She held up her hands in the universally known gesture of "What can I do?" while mouthing the word "Sorry."

Loretta clicked her tongue against her teeth, making a tsk-tsk sound. "Who styles your hair?" she asked in a disgusted huff. "And do they use scissors or a dull knife?"

"Scissors," he replied cautiously. "As to who… Different people, I guess. I just hit a QuickCuts every so often."

Melanie snickered from across the room. "Ooh, wrong answer. That's about to change," she said. "But Mom, as much as I hate interfering here, we did invite Jace to dinner."

"That's right, we did." Backing off from Jace, Loretta placed her hands on her hips. "I'll be doing your hair from here on out."

"Yes, ma'am," he replied instantly, knowing better than to argue with the mother of a woman he was interested in. "Whatever you say."

"However, you two will have to get through dinner without me." Loretta slung her purse over her shoulder and faced Melanie. "I got a phone call while you were talking with Jace, dear. It seems I have an unexpected date for the evening. Lock up when you leave, but keep the living room lights on. And *don't* worry."

Melanie darted a glance toward Jace before focusing on her mother. "You're going out? Already? Don't you think you need a little more time to recover?"

Jace couldn't see Loretta's face, but when she spoke, he

heard the anticipation sparkling in her voice. "You've always been such a worrywart. But this is going to be a good night, so you can stop fretting. I promise I'll tell you all about it tomorrow."

Every part of Melanie's face crumpled. In concern or anxiety or a mix of both, he couldn't say. "Be careful, Mom. I'll… Call me when you get home if you need an ear."

Mother and daughter hugged. Loretta whispered something that Jace couldn't hear, but a scarlet flush appeared and spread like wildfire across Melanie's cheeks. "You two have fun!" Loretta said before letting herself out.

Visibly rattled, Melanie sort of wobbled, sort of fell into a chair. "I can't believe she's putting herself through this already."

"Putting herself through what? She seemed happy and excited." Jace closed the distance between them and took a seat in the other chair.

"Love," Melanie said with an extra-large helping of venom. "Not only is it the theme of our article, but it's the theme of my mother's entire life. A life that she's spent searching—" Then, as if realizing she'd said more than she intended, she clamped her jaw shut. Hard.

Jace stared at her while warring with himself. Push Melanie into sharing whatever was going on in her head, or keep his mouth closed? If he could get her to open up anywhere, it would be here, in a place where she felt comfortable. And she was obviously distressed. He'd like to think he could be of help. On the other side of that, it should be up to Melanie to decide where—if anywhere—this conversation should go.

Every one of his muscles thrummed with the potent need to do *something*. But he didn't know what something was the *right* something. What was his goal? Getting information or helping Melanie feel better? Both if possible, but if he were forced to choose? The answer hit him like an arrow to the chest.

Going on instinct, he said, "Mel? What do you need from me right this second?"

"I don't know," she said in a fatigued, almost wooden voice. "I'm tired, I guess. Worried."

"Should I leave?" He certainly didn't want to, but he would if she answered in the affirmative. Even so, he was already planning what lame excuse he'd use when he called her from home to check in. Sleep would be impossible unless he knew she was okay.

"I don't know," she repeated. "I guess we could talk about work.... No, I don't want to talk about work. I just... Damn it! I feel like I'm the mother here, the way I worry about her."

"You love her," he said. "Why wouldn't you worry?"

"She just keeps making the same mistakes, over and over."

"Do you want to talk about that? I'm happy to listen."

Heaving another breath, Melanie shook her head. "I really don't."

"Okay," he said. "We don't have to talk at all, Mel. We could eat some dinner, watch an hour or two of mindless television, and call it a night. Or I can leave. Whatever you want."

She bolted to her feet. "Oh, no. Dinner. It has to be ruined by now."

"So we'll make something else. No biggie."

He was all set to be shown to the door, but instead she nodded. "All right. Dinner and TV. I'm surprised you don't have something better to do tonight. None of your ladies are waiting by their phone for a call?"

"At the moment, the only ladies in my life are my mother and sister-in-law," he said quietly. "Are you ever going to—" He stopped, shook his head. Now wasn't the time. "No one is waiting for me," he finished. "So let's see about the food."

The spaghetti was trashed. They settled for burgers, which Melanie topped with all the fixings. A salad appeared seemingly out of thin air, and Jace's entire contribution to the meal was opening a bag of potato chips and pouring each of them a glass of wine.

Plates in hand, they retraced their steps to the living room and found an atrociously bad horror movie to watch. Not many women appreciated the glory of a bad horror film, but Melanie did. Something that both surprised and pleased him. They batted comments back and forth about the far-fetched plot, subpar special effects and off-the-wall dialogue. Other than that, though, they didn't attempt to hold a conversation. It was easy and relaxed, almost jarringly so.

At the end of the evening, when it was time to head out, he said, "So, tomorrow. I have some research planned for the morning. I'm going to call Kurt and let him know we won't be in, that we're working in the field. That way, you can stay here tonight to talk with your mom, and we can meet up sometime tomorrow afternoon. Does that work for you?"

"That would be really helpful." Covering her mouth, Melanie yawned. "Where are we meeting and when?"

"Just give me a call whenever you're set tomorrow, and we'll take it from there." He opened the door and shivered at the blast of cold wind that met him face-first.

"Will do. And Jace? Thanks for hanging out tonight. It was nice." Her voice, sleepy and warm, forced him to turn around. To look at her.

"Welcome," he said, his voice strangely tight. "Your mom whispered something to you right before she left. What was it?"

Hesitating, Melanie sucked her lower lip into her mouth. One second was all he'd need to pull her to him for a kiss. As if she could read his thoughts, a slow, sensual smile emerged. The fire returned, both in her eyes and on her skin.

"Normally," she said in a slow, sultry tone that he'd never before heard from her, "I wouldn't tell you this, but you've been a nice guy tonight. Nicer than I expected. So, if you promise never to bring this up again—"

"I promise. Cross my heart. Hope to die. Whatever it takes."

"Okay, so here goes." She did that lower-lip suckle again, and he ceased to take in air. "My mother seems to think I need a night of great sex. And she seems to think you're the man to give it to me."

With that, she gave the door a solid push, it slammed shut, and Jace somehow managed to stumble to his car. For a parting shot, it was a damn good one. So good, he'd be awake all night thinking about the possibilities. His groin tightened as one possible image came to mind.

Hell. He might never sleep again.

Chapter Four

Melanie strode up the steps to her duplex and stabbed her key into the lock. Without intending to, she'd stayed the night at her mother's. Worry had kept her there, and fatigue had put her to sleep somewhere around three-ish. She hadn't awakened until Loretta finally decided to come home at six.

Twisting the key, Melanie pushed the door open with far more force than necessary and nearly tripped over a red gift-wrapped present that had been left on her front porch. Over the past month, she'd received two gifts wrapped in the same paper and delivered in the same way. Most likely, this one wouldn't have a card attached, either. Intrigued and annoyed, she swore under her breath, swept the package into her free arm and entered her living room.

Soft, buttery-cream-painted walls surrounded her, giving her a shot of serenity she desperately needed. Home. Finally. She loved being here more than anywhere else. Tossing the present on her secondhand, slip-covered sofa, she went to the kitchen to start a pot of coffee, hoping the caffeine would dull the pounding headache her mother's news had created.

Engaged. Her mother had agreed to marry the man who'd dumped her less than a week ago. The entire situation was ludicrous and in all likelihood would end in heartbreak. Of course, Mom didn't see it that way. No, she'd fluttered around in excitement, full of wedding plans as she showed off her diamond ring and waxed poetic about her romantic evening. When Melanie's response hadn't lived up to Loretta's expectations, mother and daughter had one of their rare arguments.

Maybe that was where the headache came from, Melanie admitted. She hated fighting with her mom. But come on… like she was supposed to believe the lame story Mr. Wade Burlington fed her mother? In his words, he'd only broken up with Loretta over fear at the depths of his feelings. Once they spent five miserable days apart, he realized how much he loved her. Hence the proposal.

All hogwash, in Melanie's opinion. Or, even if Wade spoke the truth, what was to stop him from becoming overwhelmed by fear again? Perhaps, Melanie thought with horror, at the wedding altar? Oh, God. This was absolutely going to end badly, but she couldn't do a damn thing but wait for the inevitable.

She paced the kitchen while the coffee brewed. How long would it take her mother to recover from a broken engagement? None of Loretta's other relationships had made it to the engagement stage, though a few had gotten close. What if Wade held firm until all the wedding plans were complete and then decided he couldn't go through with it? Then Mom's heart wouldn't only break: it would shatter.

The second the coffee was ready, she filled her cream-and-sugar-prepared mug, returned to the living room and collapsed on her sofa. It wasn't yet nine, so she had time to wake up and take a long, hot shower before phoning Jace.

Ugh. Collaborating on the love article wasn't going to help her current mood any. She swallowed a large gulp of coffee and sighed. She was wrong. There wasn't enough caffeine in the world to wake her up or lift her spirits today, let alone get rid of a headache.

Jace would likely have questions about her behavior last night; questions she didn't care to answer. What with her coolness at the door and the way she'd shut down after her mom had left, she was surprised he'd even stuck around. A small trickle of pleasure warmed her on the inside. He *had* stuck around, though, when he didn't have to, and he hadn't pushed even one of her buttons.

She'd enjoyed herself, she realized with a shock. Even with her anxiety over her mother, she'd found Jace's company soothing and…somehow, exactly what she needed.

It didn't mean anything, naturally. The guy knew how to be nice when the situation called for it. So what? She'd never thought of Jace as cruel. Maybe he was a little—okay, a lot—free with his affections, but he'd never been mean to her. So why did she feel unbalanced, as if the tempo of their relationship had altered into something more meaningful than before?

She didn't want meaningful with Jace. She didn't want him in on the personal beats of her life. Distance was what she wanted. She should've sent him home last night when he offered. If there was a next time, she wouldn't make the same mistake.

Her stomach clenched when she caught sight of the red-wrapped gift resting on the other side of the sofa. This was the third such present that had shown up on her front porch over the past several weeks. If this gift was like the others, it wouldn't have a card attached, and the item would be something that only a person who knew her could've chosen.

The first present, which arrived a week or so before

Christmas, had been an antique doll dating from the 1920s. Melanie didn't exactly collect antique dolls, but she had a few her mother had given her when she was a child, from before her dad left, and she liked them. But who knew that other than her mother and maybe Tara, she couldn't say.

Then, last week, the second gift appeared: a signed copy of *Charlotte's Web,* one of her favorite books from her childhood. When she'd checked online, she found that both the doll and book were valued in the one-to-two-hundred-dollar range. At that point, she didn't know if she should be flattered, annoyed or worried.

And now this. She eyed the package, downed another large swallow of coffee, and tried to decide if she wanted to open it now or wait until later. Opening the presents always gave her a strange mix of emotions: pleasure that someone had thought of her and knew her well enough to choose an item she'd appreciate, worry about who that someone was and if she should be looking over her shoulder for a potential stalker, and, not that she'd admit it to another living soul, but a tingling sense of excitement at the possibility that the gifts came from a man who found her attractive but, for whatever reason, was too shy to approach her one-on-one.

That bothered her, the fact that a bit of potential romanticism gave her a zing. It shouldn't. She had no plans of combining her life with a man's. Ever.

After draining the rest of her coffee, she set the mug on the end table and picked up the present. Might as well open the dang thing now. Procrastinating wouldn't change what the gift was or how she would feel upon opening it.

As always, she weighed the present in her hands, trying to guess what the contents might be. It felt like a book. Another signed copy of one of her favorites? Again, the odd combination of emotions overtook her. She sucked in a deep breath and ripped off the paper. Nope, no card. One look at the gift—it *was* a book—brought forth a hard tremble.

Alice in Wonderland, a book from which her father had read a few pages a night to her, nearly every night, before he'd taken off.

With a trembling hand, she flipped through the opening pages looking for a signature, because a signed copy of *Alice in Wonderland* would likely be worth megamoney. She expelled a sigh in relief when she didn't find the author's scrawl. If some anonymous person had spent thousands of dollars on her, she'd be seriously creeped out.

Still, the book was in fairly good condition and seemed to be rather old. Not a first printing, thank goodness, but probably worth a decent chunk even without the signature.

Clasping the book tightly, Melanie closed her eyes and leaned against the couch cushion. In the snap of a finger, she saw herself as a child snuggled up in bed with her tall, strong father sitting next to her. His voice, so long absent from her life, whisked into her memory as she recalled him reading *this* story to her. A story her mother had argued wasn't really a children's story at all, but Melanie had loved it, anyway. Had loved the time spent with her father each night before sleep.

Her heart thumped hard against her breastbone. She'd been wrong. These gifts weren't from a secret admirer, and they weren't about romancing her. They had to be from her father. Nothing else made sense, based on the fact that the presents all reflected periods from her childhood. But why? Was he trying to soften her up before attempting a reconciliation? That thought sent another series of trembles skittering through her, along with the hot flash of anger.

If David Prentiss somehow thought reconciliation was possible, then he had another think coming. Nothing would propel her to forgive him, to let *him* slither back into her life twenty years after he'd dumped her and her mother as if they were nothing more than trash.

Oh, God. What if he decided to approach Mom? She'd always said David Prentiss had been the great love of her life. Would she take him back now? Probably not, seeing how she was currently engaged to someone else. But her father might see that as enough reason to get in touch, if he somehow learned about the engagement. Melanie couldn't allow that. It would hurt her mother far too much.

Somehow, she was going to have to deal with this.

Later that afternoon, Melanie entered the coffee shop in downtown Portland that she and Jace had agreed to meet in. A quick search of the busy room told her he hadn't yet arrived. She settled herself at a table in the back corner to wait and pulled out her laptop and notepad.

She'd looked her father up in the Portland telephone directory, with no luck. Which meant he was either unlisted or had moved out of the city. Unlisted was more likely. He wouldn't be able to consistently drop off gifts if he lived too far away. Unless whatever he did for a living involved frequent travel to Portland. Hmm. That was a possibility worth considering.

What type of jobs had he held before he left? Melanie searched her memory, trying to bring those hazy days into focus, but failed. All she truly recalled was her mother's frustration with the sporadic paychecks. Maybe, if Melanie was careful, she'd be able to question her mother without offering an explanation as to why she wanted the information. She could also check one of those online, people-finding sites to see what came up.

The chair across from her scraped against the floor, startling her. "You look tired," Jace said as he dropped into his seat. "I take it you didn't get much sleep?"

"I'm fine," she said shortly. A light, almost fluttery sigh

escaped as she drank in his appearance. With his slightly tousled hair and unshaven jaw, he looked sexy as hell in that rough-and-tumble, just-crawled-out-of-bed sort of way that most men couldn't quite pull off.

He appraised her with doubt in his expression and concern in his eyes. "You're sure? Everything turn out okay with your mom?"

"No. Yes." She blinked and aimed her vision away from his. "Remains to be seen."

"Ah. I see," he said, though his tone clearly said he didn't. "Well, then I suppose we should get started. I'd like some coffee first. You want any?"

Relieved he wasn't pushing for more information, she reached for her purse. "Sure, let me give you some money—"

"On me." He stood and offered her a grin that softened the sharp features of his face. "What's your pleasure?"

"Surprise me," she said. "Since you're buying."

He ambled off, and her gaze fixated on his retreating form. Had she ever seen him wearing anything but a pair of jeans? She didn't think so, but she knew she'd never seen another man who looked as delicious in denim as Jace did. That annoyed her.

He was, after all, just a man.

But she couldn't stop herself from watching, from fantasizing, from wondering—all dangerous pastimes where Jace was concerned. She was a professional, dammit. She had no business lusting over anyone she worked with, but most especially not a womanizer like Jace.

The man in question returned with their coffees. He slid hers over to her and retook his seat before unbuttoning his thick, charcoal-colored flannel shirt. He tugged the shirt off, revealing a short-sleeved, black T-shirt beneath. "It's a little warm in here."

"Yes," she murmured, trying not to stare. "Warm." His

arms were firm and muscular. Not bulging, but lean and strong. If she had to guess, she'd say he'd earned his physique the old-fashioned way—from working and playing hard, and not from hours spent in a gym.

Her fingers curled around her cup in defense of the want to reach over and touch him. To feel the smooth strength of his biceps, the hard plane of his chest beneath the softness of his shirt. Dear God, she was in trouble. Her eyes fastened on to his, and she gulped for air.

"You're just a man," she blurted in an echo of her earlier thoughts. Embarrassment, rich and thick coated the back of her throat. "Like—um—any other man."

Surprise caused him to blink. "I am a man," he agreed cautiously. "But I'd like to think I'm unique. Special in my own way."

"Well, yeah. I can see that," she said, deadpan, in the dual hope of recovering her balance and pulling herself out of the hole her loose tongue had dug. "You're a Snuggie guy. I'd definitely say the term *special* applies."

Shaking his head in frustrated humor, Jace opened his laptop and powered it on. "You'll never let me forget about the damn Snuggies, will you?"

"With the photo shoot I have planned? Never." Pleased that they were on somewhat normal ground, she grinned and held up her takeout cup. "Thanks for this. What'cha get me?"

"Welcome. It's a cinnamon something or other." He cleared his throat and combed his fingers through his black-as-night hair. The combined actions spoke of a nervous vulnerability that didn't make sense. "I thought we could nail down a couple of loose ends."

"That's why we're here," she said, trying to figure out what Jace could possibly be nervous about. "What's up?"

"For starters, we need to determine how many couples we

want the article to focus on. It's always good to have a goal in mind early in the process."

"However many are necessary for me to win the bet," she said in part jest, part seriousness. "Other than that, I'm not particular."

"I could say the same," he retorted. "But I was thinking three. Say, one couple who are engaged or newly married, one couple who are five or ten years in, and one who have been together for decades."

"That sounds good."

He flashed her a grin, once again the cool, collected guy she knew. "Glad we're on the same page. Now, I guess we should toss around a few ideas of where to find our candidates."

"We could pull aside couples getting married at the county courthouse." She chewed her bottom lip in thought. "Maybe contact a few senior-citizen retirement-type groups, as well."

"Both good ideas," Jace said, typing while he spoke. "Also, I think we should interview my brother and his wife. They've been through hell and back, and are still together. I'd need to ask to see if they're willing, but—"

"No." Melanie narrowed her eyes and shook her head. "Absolutely not. The interview subjects should not be family members or friends of either of us."

"Any reason why not?"

"Unfair advantage." Mimicking one of Jace's habits, she tapped her pencil against the table. "Your brother and sister-in-law are probably lovely people, but using them for the article—in your mind, anyway—proves your side."

"Grady and Olivia are exactly the type of couple this feature is about." Jace crossed his arms over his chest. "If we talk to them, we'll only need two more couples. You're worried about the time we have available to finish the piece, correct? This will save us time."

Of course her words would come back to haunt her. Her logical side pointed out that his argument was one-hundred percent valid. If she agreed, that would mean fewer hours spent with Jace *and* fighting her suddenly sex-crazed libido. But her stubborn side refused to give in.

Using her feminine wiles, rusty as they were, she fluttered her eyelashes. "I'll agree to that if you agree to forget about the bet. That way, I only have to focus on the article."

"So you can't focus if we keep our bet in place?" Jace's mouth twitched in amusement. "Wow, Mel. I had no idea you were so worried about going out on a date with me. Afraid I'll bite?"

"N-no. Of c-course not," she stammered as the image of his mouth nibbling on her skin took control. Heat swarmed her cheeks and trickled down her neck. The faint scent of his cologne wafted over her, and it was all she could do not to lean in and inhale. Deeply.

Shoving herself as far back as she could against her chair, she frowned. "I am not worried. Nor am I afraid. What I am is competitive. You're going to have to choose, Jace. Do this my way or do it your way, but the bet goes bye-bye."

"You're blushing."

"I am not!" Flustered, Melanie rubbed at her cheeks. "It's, um, warm in here. I'm a little overheated. That's all."

"It is warm, but I'm wondering if it's that or if my comment about biting you is the culprit. I promise I don't bite… unless—" He swallowed. Hard. "Sorry. No sexual innuendo. I keep forgetting that."

Focus, she told herself. Lifting her chin, she put steel in her voice. "That doesn't surprise me. Stripes, spots…the inability to learn new tricks."

A laugh belted out of Jace. "You wouldn't be calling me an old dog, now, would you?"

"Tiger. Leopard. Old dog. Take your pick...the meanings are basically the same."

"Not really, Mel," he said with a delighted, now-I'm-having-fun grin. "The inability to change one's stripes...or spots, as the case may be...is about personality. The pieces that make up the whole of who we are, pieces that cannot be changed no matter how hard we try. But the other is more along the lines of being too set in our ways to be able to institute a successful change." He had the audacity to wink. "So you tell me, which are you accusing me of being?"

She arched an eyebrow. "As I said, take your pick. From where I'm sitting, you easily fall into both categories. There is nothing that says a person can't be both."

"You're right." His grin widened. "But you don't know me well enough to determine what traits of mine can or cannot be changed, so the stripe and spot comparison is out."

"Oh, the entire city knows you well enough to make that claim."

"As for the other...I'm not old, darlin'. And trust me when I say that I am more than willing—and capable—of learning new tricks."

She searched for a comeback and found nothing. Probably because her mind was centered on his statement...on what type of new tricks he was willing to learn. She chomped down on the inside of her mouth, thinking the pain might startle her dazed brain into coherency. When that proved unsuccessful, she swallowed a large gulp of coffee.

The rush of hot liquid burned the back of her throat, settled and refused to go down. She clamped her lips shut to stop herself from spewing coffee everywhere. Tears filled her eyes and trickled down her cheeks. She reached blindly, searching for a napkin as the coughs she couldn't contain came free. Her cheeks grew hot again, this time in embarrassment.

Jace was at her side in heartbeat. He placed his hand on her back, in the space between her shoulder blades, and rubbed in wide, firm circles. "Drank too fast, didn't you?" he said calmly, almost as if he were trying to soothe a child. "I've done that before. Sucks when it's something hot. Just give yourself a minute, and you'll be fine."

Melanie nodded and took in careful, small breaths. When she was able to talk, she said, "Some water might be good." She stared at the table, not wanting to turn toward him until she had the chance to clean herself up. "Do you mind getting me a bottle?"

His hand dropped away, and she felt his body shift. Out of the corner of her eye, she saw him walk toward the front of the coffee shop. The second she knew he wasn't going to look at her, she found the napkin and dried her face. Bemused humor replaced some of her humiliation. It was a darn good thing she wasn't trying to seduce Jace, because choking on coffee could not be described as sexy.

One little comment, and she'd forgotten how to drink. Awesome. Dabbing at her shirt, she sopped up some of the dampness and tried to work out why Jace had this…power over her. It was more than his good looks, his charm. It had to be. She'd met plenty of handsome, charming men in her lifetime. She'd dealt with relentless flirters before. She'd walked away from every single one of them without a second thought.

But Jace seemed to be of a different species. A man whose mere presence made her feel as if she'd been struck by lightning. God help her, she understood for maybe the first time in her life why women did such crazy things to get the attention of "the perfect man."

Good grief. Jace was not the perfect man. He wasn't irresistible. He couldn't be. He was nothing but a novelty. Probably, she thought, after spending the next several weeks with him, she wouldn't find him any more appealing than any other man.

Maybe, instead of trying to avoid spending time with Jace, she should be spending as much time as possible with him. Wouldn't she get used to him quicker that way? Wouldn't his...appeal...become less intense as she acclimated herself to him?

"You doing okay now?" Jace asked with a considering once-over when he returned. He handed her the water bottle and sat down. "No need to call nine-one-one or anything, is there?"

"Much better now." She unscrewed the top from the water bottle and took a careful sip. "Thank you for this. I...tend to be on the clumsy side."

A faint smile appeared. "I've noticed. How many broken bones did you have as a kid?"

"None, actually. I'm clumsy around normal, everyday objects. Like flat ground and invisible globs of air." She shrugged. "But dangerous stuff like climbing trees I never had a problem with."

"You're an interesting woman, Mel."

"In what way?" she asked, genuinely curious.

He blinked. "In every way."

"Oh." What was she supposed to say to that? "Interesting good or interesting bad?"

"Good, Mel." His voice thickened and lowered. "Very, very good."

"Oh," she said again, still at a loss for words. "Thank you. I think you're...interesting, too." Before he could quiz her on what she meant by that, she said, "Is there anything else you wanted to go over?"

"We were talking about Grady and Olivia," Jace reminded her, stubborn man that he was.

Melanie expelled a sigh. "I'd rather keep this entirely impartial."

"Why not meet them before deciding?" he pushed. "Something informal, like lunch?"

"And if I don't change my mind?"

"I'll stop badgering you, but the bet sticks." Finishing off his coffee, he crumpled the cup in his hand. "They're a special couple. I can promise that they'll be celebrating Valentine's Day because they love each other, because they choose to be together."

"Okay, okay." She decided this battle wasn't worth fighting at the moment. "I'll meet them and then decide, but I doubt doing so will change anything."

"Good enough." Jace glanced at his watch. "Crap, it's getting late. I have to take off soon, but there is one more idea I'd like to run by you."

Take off? Disappointment clouded around her before settling in her stomach like a lead weight. Where was he going? More to the point, why did she care? "Shoot," she said.

"We should publicize the bet, make it a part of the article. In addition, we could approach the feature with a 'he-said, she-said' mentality."

"Meaning?"

"We state up front that we have a bet going and what's at stake." Jace's brow furrowed as he talked. "If you win, they'll all see the damn Snuggie photo anyway. And if I win…" He trailed off and glanced away, apparently having second thoughts about completing his sentence.

"It will just play into your womanizing reputation, is that it? If anything, that will help your columns get more attention." She scowled and fought to keep her temper in check. "What then, Jace? Supposing a miracle happens and you somehow manage to win, will you use our *date* as fodder for your column?"

"I...hadn't really thought about that," he said carefully.

"Okay. Think about it now."

"No, Mel. I wouldn't 'use our date as fodder' unless that was something you'd already agreed to." The furrows in his brow deepened. "You continually assume I'm out to deceive you, in one way or another. Why?"

She let out a breath. If she was going to get through the next several weeks, she needed to relax. "I don't know," she admitted in a soft voice. "But come on, Jace, you write a dating column that is...fairly free with the details of your dates, so why wouldn't I wonder?"

"Maybe because we're coworkers? Maybe, just maybe, you could give me the benefit of the doubt for once." His eyes darkened, grew steely. "I sure as hell don't need to be sneaky about using a date for my column. *Any* date."

"Right," she fired back. "The women you date probably love having what they wear, what they say, every move they make dissected in your damn column for public consumption. Hell, they probably beg you for dates. They probably cut the column out of the paper and show it off to their friends and neighbors before framing it and hanging it on their wall."

"Some of them, maybe," Jace said quietly. "Others prefer to stay out of the limelight. Regardless, have you ever seen an actual name printed in my 'damn column'? You haven't, because I keep that information private. I respect women, Mel." He swore under his breath. "Stop expecting the worst from me."

She stared at him for a minute, letting his words filter through her temper. He was right. Sort of. To the best of her recollection, his dates were never named. Well, not with their given names, anyway. "I'll try," she said. "But I can't promise anything."

"Someday, I'm going to prove to you that I can be trusted." The sincerity in his voice caught her off guard, softened away the rest of her anger and, in a way she didn't understand, made her *want* to trust him. She shrugged and played off the moment as no big deal. "Sure, Jace. Good luck with that. Maybe you'll win the lottery, too."

He closed his eyes for a millisecond and pushed out a sigh. Then, with his playboy grin solidly in place, he put them back on familiar ground. "Anyway, if we lay the bet out right in the beginning, the readers will get involved. Actually, we should do that now as a way to get some buzz going on the article. I figure I can mention it in my columns, and you can in yours."

She nodded. "Then what?"

"Simple. We share our massively different viewpoints going in, drop in our opinions throughout—how we feel before the interviews compared to how we feel after." Jace fiddled with his crushed coffee cup and checked his watch again. "I'm fairly sure Kurt will give us the extra page space, and I know he'll like the approach."

"It's a fantastic idea," she said honestly. "Okay, if Kurt agrees, I'm in."

"I'll give him a call later to get the go-ahead." With that, Jace glanced at his watch for the third time. "I really need to get going. I'm thinking we'll start interviews on Monday."

It was on the tip of her tongue to ask where he was off to, but she managed to swallow the words. "So we're done until next week?"

"Unless I can put something together with Grady and Olivia before then, yes." Jace packed away his laptop and stood. "Have a good night, Mel. Try not to trip over any dangerous globs of air in the meantime."

"I'll try," she said, matching his light tone with one of her own. "It's hard, though. Those dang invisible air globs are everywhere."

He gave her a long, slow look, as if he wanted to say more.

In the end, he simply nodded, angled himself toward the door and strode away. She watched him again. She couldn't help it. When he exited the coffee shop, a feeling of emptiness came over her.

Surely not because Jace had left or because she wished he'd stuck around for longer. And surely not because she wondered where he was off to, if he had a date with a glamorous, non-clumsy, beautiful woman who didn't have issues about trusting men.

Feeling this way for those reasons would be stupid, and she was not a stupid woman. It had been a long day with a lot of surprises on very little sleep. Of course she was tired and out of sorts. Her meeting with Jace had been an opportunity to think about something other than her mother's engagement or her father potentially trying to become part of her life again. Jace's departure signaled the end of their meeting, and therefore a return to her earlier worries.

Yes, she decided, the cause for this sudden, engulfing loneliness wasn't because of Jace at all. His presence combined with their chat about work had simply shielded her from emotions she already had. In the absence of both, they came flooding back.

It was a good argument, she thought as she gathered her belongings, tossed her paper coffee cup in the trash and headed toward the parking lot. A valid, completely logical argument…except for one thing. Melanie wasn't thinking about her mother or her father when Jace walked out the door. No, she'd been thinking about him, that deep, almost searching look he'd just given her and his comment about proving to her that he was trustworthy.

He had been in her mind.

Now in her car, Melanie pulled the visor down to look in the mini-mirror. Her eyes were darker than normal and somewhat dazed. Her normally pale cheeks were flushed, and when she brushed her fingers down the side of her face, her skin was hot to the touch.

Oh, hell. She'd been wrong earlier, when she convinced herself that spending more time with Jace would help her get over her absurd attraction. After all, the sun's rays didn't grow less hot the longer you stood in them. All that happened then was that you got burned.

Chapter Five

Saturday afternoon, Jace was carrying a bottle of beer and a bowl of popcorn into the living room with the telephone propped between his shoulder and ear. "Thanks for getting back to me," he said to Kurt. "I'm sorry to bug you over the weekend but was hoping to get the go-ahead on this before Monday."

Kurt had been out of the office since Thursday with the flu, so Jace had finally left him a message regarding the new approach to the Valentine's Day feature. In addition, Jace wanted to have a conversation about dropping "Bachelor on the Loose" in favor of a different column.

"Look, I don't much care how you run the article. Just remember it's supposed to be a feel-good piece," Kurt said, his voice raspy.

"Right, and it will be. No problem with that. I just think the bet will draw attention, and the...let's call it contention... between me and Melanie will prove compelling."

"Like a train wreck, maybe," Kurt said. "But whatever sells papers works for me."

Jace ignored that comment, even if there was some truth there. He deposited the bottle and bowl on the end table before sitting down in his leather recliner. "I also think this format will give Melanie a better chance to show you what she can do."

Kurt responded with a grunt. "I know damn well what she's capable of. The problem is she's unwilling to follow directions. Face it, Jace, the advice column should be a cinch for anyone to write. Hell, my sixteen-year-old daughter could probably do it."

"*Unwilling* might not be the proper word." Jace popped the footrest and leaned back, looked longingly at the still-dark television. His game was about to start. "I think it's more a matter of—" This wasn't a conversation he should have with the boss. Melanie wouldn't like it. With that in mind, Jace changed tactics. "Hey, what do you think of posting a few teasers about the bet along with the feature on the *Gazette's* website for promo?"

"Sure. Shouldn't be a problem. But Jace, you should know..." Kurt hesitated a second, coughed and then said, "This is a last-shot deal for Melanie. If she screws up again, I can't give her another chance. There's too much at stake right now."

"How can the advice column be a make-or-break deal?" Jace no sooner asked the question than his intuition kicked him in the gut. "Is the paper in trouble?" Kurt's silence was all the answer Jace needed. Hell, what small newspaper wasn't struggling nowadays? "How bad is it, Kurt? Should I be looking for another job?"

"No!" Kurt coughed again. "You're fine. You're one of our most popular writers, so you're good. As long as you keep doing what you've been doing, I don't see that changing."

"Right. Keep doing what I'm doing. Great." Okay, so he wouldn't be chatting with Kurt about dropping "Bachelor on the Loose" today. Damn it. "So what's the trouble? We losing money, readers, costs too high...what's going on?"

"I'm not even supposed to be talking about this."

"Aw, come on, Kurt. You can't drop that kind of news without giving me the entire story." Besides which, Jace could tell that Kurt wanted to talk about it. "I'll keep it to myself."

Those seemed to be the magic words, because Kurt said, "We're not in trouble. Not exactly. But we might be sold soon, and the potential new owners tend to make heavy changes once they've taken over." Kurt sighed. "A lot of us won't have jobs at the end of it, or we'll be kept just long enough for them to hire replacements. I need everything to run smooth, Jace. And that includes Melanie and her column. You see where I'm going with this?"

"Yeah." Kurt was worried about his job and how Melanie's column might reflect on him. The guy had a family, had been with the *Gazette* for going on fifteen years. Jace understood, all right. Blowing out a breath, he said, "I'll do my part."

"Make sure Melanie does hers."

"Sure. Well, I'll try." They talked for another few minutes before Jace said, "Hope you're feeling better soon, Kurt."

After hanging up, Jace sat motionless and stared straight ahead, absorbing the news that the *Gazette* might be sold. He wasn't stupid. With this hanging over Kurt's head, there was no way he'd approve of Jace ending the column. Jace could leave the *Gazette,* accept one of those other offers that came in a few times per year, but the idea didn't appeal.

For one, he'd far prefer to continue living in Portland. For two, every one of those offers came with the expectation that Jace would bring "Bachelor on the Loose" with him if he accepted. And that was out of the question.

When he'd originally started the column, he had been what he wrote: a bachelor living a semi-wild life and sharing his dating adventures with the residents of Portland. The column had taken off almost immediately, something that had both surprised and empowered Jace. He'd be a liar if he stated he hadn't relished the attention or the notoriety he'd received.

Hell. What young guy, only a few years out of college, wouldn't love the attention of beautiful, single, sexy women? Of having however many dates he wanted and then having the opportunity to write about those dates to an ever-increasing audience?

In the beginning, he'd worked hard to instill the column with humor about the dating game: the chase and conquer, the thrill of never knowing when an evening began exactly where—or how—it would end. And the women were... fascinating and complex. Able to beguile a man one second and crush the same man's ego in the next, if they so chose.

Women were powerful. True, some were more attuned to their innate power than others, and there were the few here and there who—like superheroes gone bad—chose to misuse their power. He'd always found women enthralling. Captivating. And he'd loved writing about them. But he hadn't lied to Melanie. He'd never identified a woman by name. Instead, he came up with a method to—for lack of a better term—*brand* the women he dated by type.

He used ice cream flavors.

Strawberry, for example, was his classification for a fun-loving and easygoing woman, while vanilla was the perfect description for the girl-next-door type. If he wrote that he'd spent his evening with a luscious lemon, that meant the woman fell on the flirty side of the equation. Chocolate meant exotic, perhaps even a little—or a lot—spicy. And he saved rocky road for females who, for whatever reason, were just plain difficult to get along with.

His mother hated the ice cream thing. She said it was demeaning, and maybe, Jace admitted, she was right, though he'd never intended that to be the case. In truth, many of the women asked right off what ice cream flavor he saw them as. Most of them were fine with whatever he said, though he learned fast not to tell a rocky road to her face that she was, in his opinion, a rocky road. That spelled disaster with a capital *D*.

And in one case, a full glass of wine dumped over his head and a stinging slap across his cheek.

Somewhere along the line, though, Jace changed from the bachelor who loved to be one to the guy who yearned for more. He wanted stability. He wanted to settle down. With one woman on his arm, in his bed, in his life. The nonstop dates with a variety of women began feeling like a chore instead of an adventure. Actually writing the column became a burden.

He went to Kurt then and asked to drop the column, but the boss had refused. Oh, he'd given Jace a song and dance about building the popularity of his "Man About Town" column first and told him to start branching out into other areas. That they'd revisit the idea in a few months.

So Jace had played along and continued to date a different woman, sometimes two or three women, every week. That nonsense had stopped over a year ago. And the last time he'd talked to Kurt about ending "Bachelor on the Loose," Kurt hadn't bothered with the song and dance. He'd flat-out refused.

Since then, every last word in the column was fiction. Which was fine. Or had been, until Melanie stumbled into his life. Now he hated the reputation the column had given him. Obviously, much of her false opinion of him was based on that reputation, on his supposed dating escapades, on the fact that he used ice-cream flavors to describe women's personalities. She saw him as a cad. A player.

And he had no one to blame but himself.

Jace sighed and grabbed his now-lukewarm beer, gulping down a large swallow. Melanie's opinion likely wasn't going to change as long as she thought he was jumping from one woman to the next with barely a breath in between. He could come clean with her, but he doubted she'd believe him. Hell, if he stood in her shoes, he wouldn't believe it, either. And if she thought he was lying, wouldn't that just deepen her distrust of him?

Besides which, telling her the truth about the column felt like cheating. Maybe it was the trademark Foster stubbornness at play, or maybe he was too prideful, but he wanted her to learn who he was naturally, as they spent time together, and hopefully form an opinion that had zilch to do with that damn column.

Basically, he wanted her to forget every last thing she thought she knew about him and trust in what he showed her. But for that to be successful, she'd have to be willing to open her eyes and really look at him. And what were the chances of that happening?

Jace grabbed the remote and turned on the game. Maybe he'd tell her the truth. Maybe he'd wait and see. Or maybe he'd give up on the idea of Melanie Prentiss and find a woman who didn't need so much convincing.

It wouldn't be hard. He could think of several women who'd drop whatever they were doing to spend the evening with him. All he'd have to do was pick up the phone. That wasn't the issue, though. The real problem was that the only woman he wanted to call was Melanie.

Melanie and Tara stared at the computer screen, scanning through the entries the people-finding website had emailed after receiving their fifty-dollar fee. Outright robbery in Melanie's mind, as the information delivered didn't even take up a full page.

"Are you sure this David Prentiss is your father?" Tara asked. "I mean, the age looks right, but your dad doesn't exactly have an uncommon name."

"You'd think the name was common, wouldn't you? But there aren't any David Prentisses in the telephone book. Besides, this is him. Unless there is another guy with the same name and the same birthday." Melanie pointed at the date. "April fifteenth, tax day."

"I didn't even see that. You're right, this must be him."

"Uh-huh, but I was hoping for more." A neon sign with a glowing arrow leading directly to her father would've been convenient. Melanie sighed and tried to make sense of the little data in front of her. He'd declared bankruptcy a few years back, but she didn't see how that knowledge was going to be of any help. There were three residences listed, homes he'd supposedly owned over the years, but none of them were tagged as being his current residence. The two most recent had three other names listed as being a part of the household, all three of which carried the Prentiss name. "I'm guessing he remarried and had more kids."

"Looks that way," Tara said softly. "I'm sorry, Melanie. That's rough."

Melanie scowled and pushed away from her desk. "Well, if he's all happy with a new family, why is he bringing me presents?" Bitter disappointment edged her words. Somehow, she'd assumed that her dad had remained unattached. After all, if one family wasn't good enough for him, why would she think he'd take on another? "He obviously isn't lonely."

"Just because he has a family doesn't mean he can't be lonely. Or want to fix things with you. The two are not necessarily connected, and people change." Tara scrunched her nose in thought. "But honestly, Melanie, you have no idea if it is your father bringing you gifts. It could be anyone. It could be a secret admirer, like we originally thought. Or, um, I don't know, maybe it's your mother trying to make you think it's a secret admirer. I can see Loretta doing something like that. She thinks *you're* lonely."

"Mom doesn't do anything halfway. If she was behind this, the gifts would be more romantic in nature." Reaching over, Melanie made sure there was paper in her printer before sending the document to print. "I'll look at this more later, maybe see if I can track down some of his old neighbors, but right now I'm hungry. Feel like ordering a pizza?"

"Sure," Tara said agreeably, following Melanie out of the bedroom and down the stairs. "Why are you so certain you don't have some sweet, shy guy enamored with you?"

Melanie snorted. "Because if I did, he'd have to have an inside track to my childhood. It isn't like I go around spouting off what my favorite books are from when I was a kid, or that I own a couple of antique dolls."

"You're kidding, right?" Tara plopped her tall, thin frame on the couch the second they entered the living room. "All he'd need was ten minutes with Loretta to get that type of info. She chats about you nonstop at the salon. Last time I was there, I overheard her reminiscing about how you won the local spelling bee three years running."

Kneeling, Melanie dug out the pile of coupons she kept stashed under the end table. "Good grief, I was in grade school then."

"That's what I'm saying."

"Okay, but she probably got on that topic because her customer brought up spelling bees first. Mom likely asked how the family was, and the client mentioned her son or daughter was going to be in a spelling bee, or had just been in one."

Gathering the coupons, Melanie moved to the chair across from Tara. "You know how that goes."

"And what if a customer mentioned he bought a copy of *Charlotte's Web* for his niece for her birthday or for Christmas? Or that his sister collects antique dolls? See where I'm going with this?" Excitement sparkled in Tara's hazel eyes. "I believe I've proven my point. You *could* have a secret admirer. And that idea is so much more fun than dealing with your lame-o, doesn't-deserve-to-know-you father."

"I don't know about more fun, but it would certainly be less emotional. And I suppose you're right. I'll…I guess I'll call Mom later and see if she remembers talking about any of this with any of her clients." And try to find a way to bring her father into the conversation. Regardless of how much sense Tara made, Melanie couldn't rule out her dad.

"Did you ever tell Loretta about the gifts?" Tara asked.

"I haven't mentioned them, but only because I don't want to worry her."

"I doubt she'll be worried. Ecstatic is more likely." Tara's wide mouth split into a megawatt smile. "She wants grandbabies, you know."

"She should've had a couple more kids, then." Melanie flipped through the pile of coupons until she found the one she was looking for. Glancing over at her friend, she asked, "Are you a vegetarian this week?"

Tara's ash-blond hair tumbled forward as she nodded. "Going strong for a month now! But we can do halfsies if you insist on contaminating your body with meat."

Melanie laughed. "And that comes from the girl who ate nothing but cheeseburgers all through college."

"I've found I get almost the same satisfaction from a well-made veggie burger. And those days were a long time ago." And then, as if to drive in the point she made earlier, Tara said, "People change."

"Well, you haven't become a vegan when I wasn't looking, have you? Because I was thinking mushroom and cheese pizza, and I can put together a salad to go with." When Tara agreed, Melanie placed the order.

Later, after dinner was consumed and Tara had headed home, Melanie stared at the phone. She should call her mother now and get it over with, but they hadn't spoken since their argument on Wednesday morning. There would definitely be a rehash of that conversation, and Melanie didn't want to get into another fight.

She recognized that her inability to find any happiness for her mother's news was unfair, and that Loretta deserved—if nothing else—a sincere congratulation from her daughter. But she wouldn't lie. Yes, she'd be thrilled to see her mom happy, and if that meant marriage, then so be it—as long as it was with a guy who would stick. And really, who was she to say that Wade Burlington wasn't going to stick? He might. Melanie had doubts, but she'd never met the guy, so yeah, she was being unfair.

She punched in the number and stifled a groan when Mendelssohn's "Wedding March" sounded off in her ear. "Nice song, Mom," Melanie said when Loretta answered. "Is that what you're going to walk down the aisle to?"

"I haven't decided yet." Loretta took in a quick breath. "I love you, my darling girl, but if you've called to try to talk me out of this, then…don't. I'm happy, and I intend to stay that way."

"Actually, Mom, I called to apologize."

"You don't have to apologize, Melanie. You just have to believe that I know what's best for me, and support my decisions. That's all I'm asking from you."

"That's fair." Emotion curled in the back of Melanie's throat. "I really am happy that you're happy. I love you, and

I worry, and I'm sorry about that. But of course I support you. Always, Mom."

"Oh, sweetie, I'm so relieved to hear that. I...I don't know what I'd do if you couldn't...wouldn't...be at my wedding. I need you there. I was hoping that maybe..." Loretta's voice trailed off, as if she wasn't sure if she should continue.

"You were hoping what?"

"You need to meet Wade, that's all. And I know you'll adore him once you do. He's a good man, Melanie. A really good man."

Right. A good man who ran in the other direction out of fear and then came crawling back with a diamond ring and a marriage proposal. That didn't sound so good to Melanie. It sounded like the desperate actions of a wishy-washy man. But what she said was "Name the date, place and time, and I'll be there."

"I didn't think it would be that easy," Loretta admitted, her tone hushed. "I was sure you'd give me a dozen excuses why you couldn't. Thank you for not turning this into a battle."

"He's going to be your husband, which means he's going to be a part of my family. Why did you think I wouldn't agree to a meeting?"

"Don't play that game, Melanie Ann. Why, you've refused to meet any of the men I've had relationships with ever since you moved out of the house."

"You weren't marrying any of them. This is different." Melanie paced while they talked, listening to her mother but also thinking ahead to the rest of the conversation she wanted to have. "Look, Mom, I'm sorry for the other day, and I'm sorry for...for making you think I'm not interested in this. I am. I only want the best for you, and if the best is Wade, then I'm glad you found each other."

"Do you mean that?"

"Yes."

"Oh, honey, this is marvelous news! Think of all the fun we'll have planning the ceremony! You can help me find my wedding dress…I'm thinking semiformal. Maybe a shorter hemline to show off my legs. And we'll have to find a dress for you." Loretta sighed in pure contentment. "Now I can really be excited."

Melanie closed her eyes and swallowed the words that were crowding her mouth. Words that would propel them into another argument and would solve less than nothing at this point. "Let's just focus on the get-together first. This, um, isn't real for me yet, because I don't have a, um, mental image of Wade. So yeah, meeting him is a great idea."

"That makes sense. How can you advise me on the perfect wedding dress when you haven't even seen what the groom looks like?" Whew. Mom was so relieved to hear what she wanted to hear, she hadn't clued in on Melanie's hesitation. Thank goodness. "Wade and I are spending the day together tomorrow, since the salon is closed on Sundays. I'll find out what his schedule looks like, and we'll set something up as soon as possible."

"Good. That's good. I'm…looking forward to it." Sending a silent prayer upward that she handled this next bit well, Melanie said, "One other thing, Mom. Tara and I hung out today, and we got on the subject of Dad. It made me realize how little I remember about him."

Loretta was quiet for a few seconds. "You were only seven when David left. I'm surprised you remember anything at all."

"Some things. I remember how he'd read to me every night. I remember that he loved your lasagna. And, um, I remember he always seemed to have a different job." Mentally crossing her fingers, Melanie said, "But I can't recall what types of jobs he actually had. Do you remember any of the places he worked?"

"Well, goodness, Melanie, what an odd question. Why would you care about something like that?" Loretta gasped. "Is this about Wade? Sweetheart, no one can replace your father. If you're thinking that Wade is going to try to—"

"Mom, no. Jeez, that so isn't what I'm getting at. I...don't even consider David Prentiss as my father anymore. He's just a man I barely remember. And I'm certainly not worried about Wade—or anyone—trying to replace Dad. I'm twenty-seven years old. I've outgrown the need for a father."

"You may not need a father, but I'm sure you wish you had one. If I could change one aspect of your life, it would be this."

"I'm fine. Really," Melanie said quickly. "I'm just curious about what types of jobs Dad held. That's all."

Again, Loretta went silent, obviously lost in the past. When she spoke, it was with a quiet resolve. "I've waited a long time for you to ask me questions about this, but I expected you to be curious about why he left, about what happened. You've never asked."

"He left, never came around again and that's all I need to know on that." Okay, perhaps not the complete truth, but this was a conversation they shouldn't have over the freaking telephone.

"Well then, honey, I guess I'm a little confused. Why do you care about your father's employment history?"

Thinking on her feet—literally—Melanie said, "Well, you know that Tara is a teacher. So is her father. And Tara and her dad have a lot of other things in common. Like...um—" Crap. Truthfully, other than their careers, Tara and her dad were polar opposites. "Fishing. They both love to fish!" Lie. Tara would rather have her teeth pulled out one by one than spend the day with worms dangling off the end of a fishing pole. "So, you know, I started to wonder if I had anything in common with Dad. Like, maybe writing?"

"David wasn't a writer. You get that from my mother, God rest her soul. I wish you had a chance to know her, Melanie. Talk about someone you have a lot in common with! Why—"

"So, what type of work did Dad do, then?" Melanie interjected, knowing how easily her mother could get off target. Besides, she'd heard all the stories about her maternal grandmother before, and yes, she'd like to hear them again. Just not now.

"Oh, anything and everything. Let's see... He spent some time as a car salesman, and then he worked at an insurance agency, selling life insurance. He tried his hand at security for a while." Loretta laughed, but Melanie didn't think from humor. More like exasperation. "He was a repo man for a few months. That job was hell. Oh, I know. The one profession he'd always fall back on was bartending. Used to say that someday, he was going to own a bar."

"Wow," Melanie said as her mind absorbed that information. "He really did do a little of everything."

"Yes. David had—still has, I'm guessing—a short attention span. I used to call it the 'shiny new job syndrome,' because he never lasted more than six months, no matter the job. The next one always looked better to him."

"But he wanted to own a bar?" To Melanie, that seemed an odd aspiration. "What was the reasoning?"

"Your dad loved being around people. He was good around them, too. Had a way about him that made folks comfortable. He could get anyone to laugh." Loretta's tone dipped as her memories got the better of her. "It never mattered how angry I was at that man, he could always make me laugh. We laughed a lot for a long time, Melanie. Until we stopped."

Her mother's voice was broken, hesitant and very near tears. Melanie decided to drop the subject. She'd learned a little. Maybe she'd be able to learn more later. "Thanks for sharing."

"You're welcome. All you ever have to do is ask. I... Is there anything else you're curious about?"

While Melanie knew her mother's question was specific to David Prentiss, the conversation with Tara popped into her head. But now wasn't the time to ask about antique dolls or childhood books. "Well, yeah," Melanie teased. "You never told me what everyone at the salon said when they saw your engagement ring."

"Oh! They all love the ring. Of course, there was some jealousy, but that's to be expected. Why, Sandra has been waiting for years for her beau to pop the question. If I've told her once, I've told her a thousand times..."

Melanie grinned, sprawled out on her sofa and listened to her mother chatter.

After thirty minutes or so, Loretta said, "You're awfully quiet, honey. Are you okay?"

"Fine. Tired, I think."

"Well, go tuck yourself in and have sweet dreams. I'll see you on Tuesday for dinner, right?"

Melanie responded in the affirmative, gave her mother her love and ended the call. Once upstairs, she pulled the printout of her father's information off the printer and scanned it again, looking to see if she'd missed anything earlier. She hadn't.

But as she stared at the tiny slice of David Prentiss's life, hurt she'd believed to be long gone blossomed as if it were new. How dare he walk out on them, only to create a new family? Before, as much as she tried not to think about her father, she'd assumed that family life simply hadn't agreed with him, so he took off.

That meant he was a coward, yes, but also had nothing to do with her seven-year-old self, or her mother. That was *his* fault. *His* weakness. Not theirs.

So this...this made her question everything she'd convinced herself to be true. This told a different story than the one she'd recited to herself every single night for those first agonizing months after he disappeared. God, she'd loved her father. Adored him, really. She wondered, briefly, what type of woman she would be if he hadn't left. What would her life be like now?

Would she have a husband, kids? Would she still be a journalist? What parts of her were the way they were because of his departure? And what parts were just her, no matter the upbringing, no matter his failure at being a father?

It ticked her off that she didn't know, would never know.

She lifted her hand to her cheek, surprised to feel the wetness of tears she hadn't realized were falling. Over him? Really? Tossing the paper aside, Melanie readied herself for bed and tried to plan her next move. Because yes, she was going to locate him, whether he was behind the gifts or not. He might not deserve her tears, but she deserved some answers.

And she damn well intended to get them.

Chapter Six

Jace swung his 1969 Camaro Super Sport, the car that his older brother Grady had rebuilt for him and painted orange, into the turn lane. With the car idling, Jace tossed a look toward Melanie but kept his thoughts to himself. She'd been strangely quiet all morning. While they were still at the office, he'd assumed she was caught up in writing next week's advice column, even though the column wasn't due until Friday.

But she'd barely said three words since they'd taken off for the county courthouse. When the light changed to green, Jace revved the engine and turned the corner. Thinking back, he realized she hadn't said much ever since their meeting last week. No sarcastic rejoinders. No narrowing of her pretty brown eyes. No calling him out in the few instances he'd slipped into flirting with her. And, even more telling, not even one mention of his Snuggies.

Instead, she'd treated him with a daunting, straight-faced

silence that, frankly, was beginning to drive him crazy. It also worried him. Melanie wasn't the silent-routine type of woman, and she never missed an opportunity to put him in his place. So, yeah, something was obviously bothering the lady.

He just wished he knew what.

Approaching the courthouse, he found an empty space alongside the curb, less than a block away. He slid the car in. "This should be fun," he said in a purposefully cheerful voice. "You brought the release forms, correct?"

"Yes." Melanie unbuckled her seat belt and leaned forward to grab her bag. "Is Jenny meeting us here? She was assigned to this, right?"

Melanie was referring to one of the staff photographers. "Initially, yes. But Kurt decided we can get the photos we need easily enough. I've taken my own shots before, and we can always arrange for follow-ups if we need more."

"Right. If we manage to find even one couple worth following up with."

"If we don't, that doesn't mean anything so early in." Jace reached behind him to retrieve his canvas messenger bag. "But you know that."

She gave a barely perceptible nod before stepping out of the car. Great. More silence.

Jace swallowed a sigh, joined Melanie on the sidewalk and belatedly remembered to feed some coins into the parking meter. She pulled her jacket tightly around her and stuffed her hands into her pockets. It was a cold, gray and windy day. Typical of January weather in Portland, though there was some talk of a possible ice storm later in the week.

"How are we going to do this?" Melanie asked as she took off toward the four-story, concrete building that had served as the county courthouse since 1914. "Does anyone know we'll be here?"

"Public venue. We don't have to get permission if we stick to the public areas. But," he said, falling in step next to her, "the weddings are by appointment only. I was worried we'd pick a day that no one would be here, so I called ahead."

"And?"

"Three judges are sitting this afternoon, and all of them have a packed schedule. Should be plenty of couples in and out."

"That doesn't mean any of them will want to talk with us," she pointed out, stubborn as always. Which actually helped set Jace's mind at ease. Maybe she was fine, after all.

"They'll be more than happy to spend a few minutes with us."

"And you know this how?" Melanie asked as they reached the front door. The wind blew a strand of hair into her eyes, and it was all he could do not to reach over and brush it away. "Do you have a Magic 8 Ball in your pocket?"

He grinned. "Nope, but I have a handful of gift certificates to area restaurants and clubs to pass out as a thank-you. I even have one from L'Auberge," he said, naming a Portland French restaurant known for its food and elegant atmosphere.

Melanie stepped into the courthouse and waited for him to follow. When he did, she turned to him with narrowed eyes. "How'd we get those? I know the paper didn't spring for them. Did you buy them?"

"Ah…no." Well, the L'Auberge one had been a gift from a female admirer, but Melanie didn't need to know that. "You forget who you're talking to here, Mello Yello."

"Just spill it. Where'd they come from?"

"I get freebies in the mail every week," he said with a shrug. "Managers and owners send them in the hopes I'll take a date there or mention them in the 'Man About Town' column. Sometimes, I return them with my apologies. Other

times, I use them but make sure they know there isn't a guar-
antee of publicity."

"Uh-huh," she said with an arched brow. "And this time?"

"I called, told each of them about the feature, promised
I'd give them a thanks on the website and asked if we could
use them as giveaways for the couples we interview. No one
objected."

"I suppose that makes sense," she said. "Thanks for…
thinking ahead."

"I want this to be successful." He nodded toward the elevators. "Ready to get started?"

"Why not?" She sighed as if the entire idea was about as
appealing as a mouthful of vinegar. "The sooner we start, the
sooner we'll be done."

Jace fought the urge to ask what the heck was bothering
her. This wasn't the time or the place. Somehow, though,
before the day ended, he was determined to discover what
was going on inside that head of hers.

They set up in the long hallway outside of the appropriate
judges' quarters. At the moment, there were three couples sitting on the benches that were placed against the walls. Jace
and Melanie claimed a vacant bench as theirs, where they
stacked the release forms, gift certificates, a couple of note-
pads and the digital voice recorders they'd brought with them.
Jace pulled his camera out of the bag and slung it around his
neck.

Speaking quietly, Melanie said, "So, um, I don't have a
lot of experience in this. I haven't done any one-on-one interviews since college." She paused and fiddled with the buttons on her fuzzy yellow sweater. The inane thought that she
looked like a sunflower popped up in his brain. A beautiful,
bright, sunny flower. "Any advice, Mr. Hotshot?"

"Wh-what?" He cleared his throat and tried to find his
bearings. "Oh. Advice. Um… Well, let's see. We don't want

to approach any of the couples waiting out here. Right now, all that's in their minds is their wedding. Once their ceremonies are over with, though, they'll be excited and relaxed. So we'll have to be ready for them when they come out of the judge's chambers." He gestured toward the closed doors. "There are probably ceremonies going on right now."

"I guessed that much. But… Oh, never mind." Melanie attached a few release forms to a clipboard and picked up a voice recorder. "I'll figure it out," she said in a strained voice.

She was nervous, he realized with a start. Well, duh. She'd pretty much said that straight-out. If he hadn't been staring at her and obsessing over freaking sunflowers, he might've caught on. He shook his head, disgusted with himself. God, he could be an idiot. "Look, this will be a breeze. We ask a few basic questions and go from there."

The door three down from where they stood opened, and a couple that Jace pegged to be in their late thirties emerged. He glanced at Melanie and grinned, aiming to put her at ease. "Here we go. How about if I take these two and you get the next?"

Melanie's complexion paled a shade, but she moved her head up and down in a loose nod. Thrusting the clipboard and voice recorder into his hands, she said, "Sure. That sounds good. I'll, um, tag along and watch."

"It'll be a breeze," he repeated, looking her directly in the eyes. "You ready?"

"Ready."

Jace plastered on a smile and ambled toward the couple. "Congratulations!" he said as way of greeting. "My name is Jace Foster, and this lovely lady is Melanie Prentiss. We're reporters for the *Portland Gazette*. Can you spare a few minutes to chat with us?"

The man, a tall brunet with a receding hairline, frowned.

"What is this about? There isn't a protest or something going on, is there?"

"No, nothing like that," Jace assured him. He gave them a quick rundown on the Valentine's Day feature. "As a thank-you, we'd love to send you somewhere special to celebrate. On us, of course."

The bride, a pretty woman with round cheeks and short, auburn hair, sidestepped her new husband and gave Jace a beaming smile. "I know who you are! You dated a past co-worker of mine once. It was several years ago, but we heard all about it at the office." She grimaced in recollection. "*All* about it. I didn't think Francesca would ever shut up, to be honest."

He shot a quick look in Melanie's direction before saying, "Ah…is that right?" He remembered the blonde, vivacious Francesca. They'd spent a long weekend together at a friend's place on the coast. By day three, she'd put down his friend, his friend's wife and even their dog. He'd never called her again. "Well, this has nothing to do with that."

"Still, it's interesting to hear about," Melanie said from her spot beside him. "What flavor did you label Francesca as?" He glanced at her again, this time with a frown, and she shrugged. "What? I can't be curious?"

"That was a long time ago, Mel," he said lightly. "I really don't recall."

"I believe you wrote that she was a chocolate who morphed into a rocky road." The bride chuckled. "That sort of ticked her off, but it made perfect sense to me."

The groom coughed to get their attention. "We really don't have time for all of this," he said with a glance at his watch. "I fit this in between meetings, so…"

Jace kept his expression neutral but cringed inside. Not a good start if the groom was in a hurry to get back to work on his wedding day. One look at Melanie told him she was having the same thoughts. Hell, this was a win for her love-doesn't-exist side if he ever saw one. Deciding not to push when there were likely other couples who would fit the tone of the article better, he returned his attention to the couple. "Of course. Thank you for—"

"Really, Geoffrey?" the bride interrupted, her voice quietly firm. She turned on her heel and placed her palm on his cheek. "I know today's meetings are important for our business, but this is our wedding day. Think how wonderful it will be to have that article to show our children someday."

Skimming her hand with his, Geoffrey said, "I know...it's just a big day." He let out a breath. "But as usual, you're one-hundred percent correct. Okay, Veronica. Fifteen minutes."

Without turning around, Veronica asked, "Will fifteen minutes give you what you need?"

"Fifteen minutes is more than enough," Jace promised.

He chanced a look at Melanie, expecting her to appear surprised that this couple might be turning out to be a love match when all prior signs had seemed to point in the opposite direction. But she had a smug expression on *her* face. Had she truly not noticed?

After several photos were taken and the release signed, Jace powered on the recorder, placed it between them on the bench, and said, "So, tell us. When and how did you two meet?"

"Oh, we were next-door neighbors. We knew each other for years before I finally asked Geoffrey on a date." Veronica tipped her head to the side, giving her husband a teasing glance. "I was tired of waiting for him to ask."

Geoffrey's cheeks reddened. "I thought you were out of my league." Focusing on Jace, he said, "I had no idea she was even interested."

"Only because you were blind," Veronica said with a faint smile. "I had to jump through hoops to get your attention."

"Tell us," Jace prodded. This was what he loved about interviews. You never knew where the most general of questions could lead you.

Now, Veronica blushed. "I started by baking him cookies, brownies, anything sweet, because Geoffrey has a sweet tooth."

"I just thought she was being nice," Geoffrey said. "Neighborly, you know?"

"And then I started doing my yard work in…well, somewhat revealing clothes." Veronica gave a slight shudder. "All that did was rouse the interest of some of the married men in the neighborhood. Geoffrey didn't even notice."

"I noticed," the groom said. "Believe me, I noticed. But why would I think you were dressing that way for me?"

"Because the only time I did yard work was when you were home. And I tended to wait until you were out in your yard doing something." Veronica shook her head in amusement. It was obvious that the bride and groom had gone over this before but still enjoyed sharing their story. "Like I said, he was blind."

Melanie leaned forward, curiosity gleaming in her eyes. "Why did you keep trying if he didn't seem interested?"

"Because I knew he was the man for me," Veronica said with conviction. "The first time I met him, it was as if everything inside of me came to life."

Those words knocked the air clean out of Jace's lungs. Yes. That was how he had felt the first time he met Melanie. Looking at Geoffrey, he asked, "What about you? Did you feel that way when you met Veronica?"

"It was like nothing I'd felt before," Geoffrey acknowledged.

"Then items started mysteriously breaking in my house. Almost every week." Veronica nudged her husband with her elbow. "Of course, I needed Geoffrey's help in fixing everything."

"I still can't believe you did that." Geoffrey shook his head, but Jace saw the mix of pride and pleasure in his gaze. "First it was her clogged garbage disposal, then it was the broken faucet, then her garage door opener fizzled. One thing after another for…three, four months?"

"Something like that. And that's when I gave up all of my games and asked him out. We sold our houses within a year and moved into a new home together." Veronica sighed in contentment. "A few months ago, we opened our own business. And last month, Geoffrey proposed, and here we are. That's our story in a nutshell."

"It's a wonderful story," Jace said. "And it's obvious how much you love each other."

"But why did you decide to get married here, instead of having a big wedding?" Melanie asked, her voice low and even. "Don't get me wrong, but this seems…sort of rushed and, well…" She trailed off and shrugged. "Not romantic at all."

"We started to plan a formal wedding," Veronica admitted. "But we were getting stressed, and our families weren't helping. Every time we turned around, they wanted to add more people to the guest list. We were beginning to dread a day that is supposed to be wonderful."

"So we decided that the wedding itself meant far less to us than actually being married," Geoffrey said. "But we're having a party for our friends and family this weekend. Today we wanted just for us."

"I see." Melanie shifted, reached for the clipboard and the other recorder. "Jace will finish up with you. I'm going to move on to another couple before any others get away from us." Standing, she gave Geoffrey and Veronica a smile that didn't quite reach her eyes. "Thank you for taking the time out of your busy day. And, um, congratulations."

Jace pretended he was okay with Melanie's departure. They were here to interview as many couples as possible, after all. Yet, he couldn't erase the suspicion that her quick-footed escape had little to do with the work that needed to be done. No, something about *this* couple's story bothered her. He was sure of it, even if he couldn't detail the reasons why.

Setting his questions aside, he returned his attention to Geoffrey and Veronica. He had five more minutes before they needed to leave, and he planned on using every second.

The next two and a half hours were filled with back-to-back interviews. Most of the couples were friendly, but there were only a handful that stood out in Jace's mind.

There was the couple who'd already been married and divorced twice—to and from each other—and was going for round number three. It was clear that they loved each other, and Jace admired their perseverance, but he had to wonder what their chances of success were.

He'd also spoken to a young couple who'd decided on a last-minute wedding because the bride had received orders for deployment, which made Jace think about his younger brother. Seth was in the air force, currently deployed in Afghanistan, and wouldn't be home for several more months. He *would* make it home, though. Jace refused to consider any other option.

Wishing the couple well, Jace gave them the L'Auberge gift certificate. Then, just before they left, unable to stop the comparisons between the young bride and his brother, he tossed in two others. He wasn't a softie, Jace assured himself. He was simply showing his support.

Through it all, he'd pause to snap a few photos for Melanie. She seemed to be on the fast track, zipping through each interview and moving on to the next in record time. There was one couple, though, that she spent considerably longer with. The bride was obviously pregnant, the groom obviously proud. Both of them were visibly nervous about their future.

When that interview was over, Melanie made a mad dash to the restroom, but not before Jace saw the dampness in her eyes and the heavy set of her shoulders. Curious and concerned, he tried to bring his current interview to an end before she reappeared. That didn't happen. When he finally managed to get away, she was already involved with another couple.

Now, they were heading back to the office. And again, she'd reverted to her straight-faced silent routine.

Jace gave her a sidelong glance. "I think we should exchange recorders and listen to each other's interviews tonight. We can chat about them tomorrow, decide who we might want to follow up with."

"Sure. I don't think any of the couples I spoke with are worth a follow-up, though." Melanie pivoted her upper body and stared out the passenger-side window. "But feel free to take a listen. Maybe I missed something."

"Hmm. What about the couple who is expecting a baby? You seemed really interested in them. I noticed you, ah, sat with them longer than any of the others."

"They were uneasy at first. Only reason I took more time with them was because they were shy. Part of my job is to make them comfortable, yes?"

"Well, yeah. Naturally. But you…" Hell, should he ask? How could he not? "You were upset when they left. Why?"

She let out a strangled-sounding laugh. "You're imagining things. I wasn't upset."

"I know when a woman is upset, Mel, and you were upset." Seeing the parking garage that the *Gazette* employees used, he slowed the car to take the turn. Dammit. He should've started this conversation the second they left the courthouse, because Melanie would likely fly from the car the instant it was stopped. "Your eyes were…shiny."

"Shiny?"

"Yeah. Like you were about to cry." He pulled the car into his spot and shut off the ignition. "Look at me, Mel. Please?"

She did, and he expected to see frustration on her face. Maybe even anger. But all he saw was confusion and hurt and an indefinable something that yanked at his heart. Hard.

"That woman is hardly more than a girl, and she's pregnant," Melanie said softly. "They got married because he knocked her up and they think it's the right thing to do."

"Do they love each other?"

"They *think* they love each other."

"Then marriage is the right thing to do." Jace absolutely believed that. "If they love each other and they're bringing a baby into this world, then marriage is the appropriate step."

"They don't know what they're getting into." Shifting, Melanie unbuckled her seat belt. "They're too young. Like barely into college young."

"Young makes most everything harder, but not impossible." Jace watched Melanie carefully, almost warily. He sensed this conversation was important. If he said the wrong thing, she would bolt. "On the other hand, most of us don't realize that until we have some life experience. We just roar in, tackling everything head-on, believing that failure isn't even an option. That can be an advantage."

"An advantage, Jace?" Melanie tipped her chin so their gazes met. "Really?"

Jace nodded, choosing to stay quiet.

"Things will be great for them at first, I'll give you that. Then the baby will be born. The baby will be loved and cherished and everything will be fantastic. Until they start worrying about money, doctor's bills, stuff the kid needs…and… and maybe they'll stick it out for a while. Maybe for years, even. Until one day, Daddy decides it's all too much responsibility, so maybe he starts thinking about how his life could've been. Maybe he takes off, leaves his wife. Leaves his child." The words poured from Melanie in a rush, each one bleeding into the next. "What happens to the kid then, Jace?"

"Whoa, Mel." Jace grasped her hand and squeezed. His brain was buzzing as he began to put two and two together. "Take a breath. You have no way of knowing—"

"I'll tell you what happens. That kid grows up wondering where her father went, wondering why he left, wondering if he ever loved her at all." Melanie shook her head, and tears pooled in her eyes. "And the wife…she'll spend *her* life trying to find love again, trying to replace the relationship she thought was going to last forever. But she'll miss him. She'll always miss him, even twenty years later."

Melanie blinked, as if surprised she'd said so much. Her tears, which she'd managed to hold back until now, slid down her face and dripped off her chin. She angrily swiped them away, but they kept coming. Jace ached to pull her into his arms, hold her tight, comfort her until she stopped crying. But he was afraid she'd run if he tried.

Instead, he brushed his thumbs along her cheeks, capturing her tears as they fell. "How old were you when your dad took off?"

"Seven," she said quietly, her brown eyes centered on his. "I never saw him again."

"No every other weekend at his place or summer trips to the lake?" Jace had to ask, even though she'd already stated she'd never seen her father again. Mostly because the idea of it just didn't compute. "Just gone?"

"Just gone," she confirmed. "And he never warned me. Never even hinted that he might not be around when I woke up. Just read a few pages from my book, like he did every night, and that was the last time I saw him."

Lacing his fingers into her hair, Jace leaned over and dropped a light kiss on her forehead. It was pure instinct to do so, and he was shocked when she didn't pull back. "I'm sorry, sweetheart. So very sorry you've carried this around with you."

"But that's just it. I haven't." She inhaled a jagged breath. "Or at least, I don't think I have. Recently, though, I've been—" She sort of shook herself. "Today, I mean. That interview… I guess it dredged up memories I thought were long forgotten."

Jace knew that wasn't the complete truth, and while he wanted to push, wanted her to trust him enough to tell him everything, he chose not to. He couldn't. Not when Melanie seemed so fragile. "That can happen. I…I had a moment today, myself."

Now she shifted away, as if suddenly realizing her close proximity to Jace. He dropped his hands to his lap, missing the feel of her immediately. She wrapped her arms around herself and asked, "Really? What, um, what happened?"

So he told her about his younger brother and how the couple with the soon-to-be-deployed bride had stirred up memories of Seth. The fear that often struck Jace out of nowhere, that his out-to-save-the-world brother might never make it home. Words poured out of Jace's mouth that he barely admitted to himself, let alone spoke to another person.

He finished with, "I respect the hell out of Seth and what he's doing, but I also hate what he's doing. Why couldn't he have chosen a safer career? One that kept him here…where I could look after him?" Jace shrugged to lessen the tension tightening his shoulders. "I mostly try not to think about it, but every now and then—like today—something or someone reminds me, and that's all it takes."

Melanie's gaze softened as she looked at him. "It's natural to worry about the people we love. I've spent most of my life worrying about my mom. Is Seth able to check in every so often?"

"Oh, yeah. He calls whenever he can, and we get emails more regularly."

"It's sweet you want to look out for him. How old is Seth?"

"Two years younger than me. Thirty-two. Why?"

"You're thirty-four?" Melanie's lips spread into a grin when he nodded. "Why, Jace, you're almost an old man."

"I am nowhere near being an old man," Jace said quickly, wanting to strike that thought out of her head right away. He knew they were seven years apart, but hell, that wasn't so much. Besides, what did age have to do with anything? "Nowhere near," he repeated.

"Okay," she said easily, though the smile remained. "But Seth is older than I am, doing what he wants to do. I doubt he needs looking after."

"He's still my baby brother. It is still my job to watch over him."

She seemed to consider that for a minute before asking, "Who watches out for you?"

"My brothers, my parents." Jace lifted his hand, ready to reach over and stroke her cheek again, but had second thoughts. This was the most honest conversation he'd had with a woman in a long, long time. Well, a woman who wasn't a relative. He didn't want to ruin it. "My sister-in-law. Hell, my entire family."

"I can't imagine what it would be like to have so many people in your corner. It's just been me and my mom for... well, nearly forever." There was a sad, almost melancholy note to her voice that struck Jace deep. "But we've managed."

Anger at a man he'd never met boiled in Jace's blood. "Your father isn't worth a second thought, Mel. You and your mom deserved a hell of a lot more. *Still* deserve more."

"Wow, Jace," Melanie said in an overly bright voice. "For

once, we actually agree on something." In a snap, the atmosphere in the car changed. Melanie leaned over to grab her bag from the floor, unzipped it and took out the digital voice recorder she'd used that day. "Let's make the switch now and get back to work. We've been out here for a while."

Yep, their conversation—and this moment—was over. "Sure," he said, retrieving his recorder. They made the exchange, and Melanie went for the door. "Wait a minute, Mello Yello. Are you okay?"

"I'm fine. I'm always fine, Jace, but thanks for asking." With that, she let herself out, gave a little wave before closing the door and headed toward the elevator.

Jace didn't move right away, and Melanie didn't look back, not even to check to see if he was following. He let the information he'd learned sift through his brain, let it merge with what he already knew about her and tried to fill in the missing pieces.

A dad who'd taken off with no warning and no explanation. A mom who, while loving and supportive of her daughter, had dated one man after another in her search to replace the husband who'd broken her heart. Melanie had said that love was the theme of Loretta's life, so that made sense. It fit.

What would those two things do to a child growing up? What would they do to the woman that child became? Jace couldn't really say. Not for sure. His family life had been rock-solid, so his life experience was vastly different from Melanie's.

But hell, it was no wonder she didn't trust men.

He hurt for her. For the child she'd been and for the woman he knew today. And, yes, the caveman in him wanted to find her father and pound some sense into him. But that was an action that needed to be taken twenty years ago. Doing so now would be pointless.

Jace exited the car and followed in Melanie's footsteps, his mind circling endlessly. He couldn't go back two decades to change what had already occurred, and he couldn't repair the damage that had already been done. But he had to do something. Every part of him screamed with the necessity of doing *something*.

God help him, he wanted to be exactly what she told him she didn't need: her hero. And, he realized as he reached his office, he'd never wanted to be anyone's hero before.

So what the hell did that mean?

Chapter Seven

Melanie hunched over her laptop and read through the draft of her column for the third time. While the piece wasn't due for a few more days, she had this itchy, almost uncomfortable sensation that it had to be perfect. No surprise given the fact she was nearly fired a week ago.

Would've been, if not for Jace. Warm tingles sped along her skin. She stole a glance toward Jace's office and lifted her hand to touch her forehead. He'd kissed her there yesterday, almost casually, as if doing so was the normal state of affairs between them. It should have ticked her off or at the very least sent her scurrying back to her side of his car.

Instead, she'd felt warm and safe and—underneath her crazy mix of emotions—electrified. So electrified that the yearning to lean in closer, to put her lips on his and steal a real kiss, came over her. She hadn't, of course. That would have been really crazy, but the thought…and the yearning… hadn't subsided.

He'd been so easy to talk to, and he'd listened. Really listened to what she had to say, even though she'd likely sounded a little off her rocker. It was confusing. How could the writer of "Bachelor on the Loose" be the same man she was beginning to know? Jace Foster played with women, took advantage of them—even if they knew what they were getting into when they went out with him—and, as far as she could tell, was nowhere close to stopping.

Yet her intuition told her to look beyond the surface. That maybe, just maybe, Jace was a heck of a lot more than she'd assumed.

Which was also nuts. How many women believed that about a man, only to find they were dead wrong? Based on the letters she received for her advice column, a hell of a lot.

Sighing, Melanie returned her attention to the column, reading through the first letter and her response again. The writer, a woman who'd been married for three years, stated that her once-passionate husband seemed to have lost all interest in sex. Melanie wanted to tell the woman that it was likely hubby hadn't lost interest in sex at all, but that he'd found a new playmate.

Naturally, she couldn't do that. Instead, she encouraged the wife to talk to her husband, to tell him how she was feeling, and to be honest about how his disinterest affected her. Then, if that didn't work, to try changing their routine by spicing up the bedroom a bit. She left it up to the woman as to what that might entail, because Dr. Ruth, Melanie was not.

The answer worked, as did her responses throughout the rest of the column. If Kurt found anything objectionable, she'd be surprised. She glanced toward Jace's office again, and that balmy, almost liquid sizzle returned. She'd barely seen him today. They hadn't yet discussed yesterday's interviews, either.

Hmm. Maybe she should have him look over the column,

just to be sure. There was nothing wrong with that. She was being nice, that was all. Letting Jace know that she appreciated his trust in her, but also respected him enough to not chance his risking his job.

Melanie printed the column before she could talk herself out of her lame argument. She knew her work hit the acceptable level. If she dissected her reasons for going to Jace, she'd end up changing her mind. And she really wanted to see him.

Grabbing the sheets of paper, she went to Jace's office and peeked in. His elbows were planted on his desk, his head bent toward his laptop and his expression one of intense concentration. Suddenly feeling foolish, she started to step away at the same second he looked up. Dark-chocolate eyes landed on her, warmed and the barest hint of a smile touched his lips.

Why did he have to be so dang appealing?

"I'm sorry to bother you," she said, focusing on keeping her voice clear and her gaze steady. "I… You look busy. I can come back later."

"One, you're never a bother, Mel." He raked his fingers through his shaggy hair, an action she was beginning to notice he did quite often, and then gestured for her to enter. "Two, I could use a break. What's up?"

Stopping just shy of the chairs flanking his desk, she held out the printed pages of her column. "I was wondering if you could review this? I worried nonstop last week that there would be a problem, and I'd, um, just feel better if I had a second opinion this week."

Surprise and relief colored his expression. She'd expected the surprise, but the relief annoyed her. Just a little. Still, he hesitated before agreeing. "You're sure?" he asked. "I don't want you to feel obligated to do this. We have an agreement."

"I'm sure. Besides, you also have an agreement with Kurt. I'd say that trumps ours," Melanie said, going for levity.

"*Nothing* trumps anything to do with you."

Her annoyance evaporated. "That's...nice, but you shouldn't have to worry about your job over this. I was upset last week and..." She shrugged off the rest of her statement, not ready to admit her opinion of Jace wasn't quite the same as it had been a mere seven days earlier. She placed the printed sheets on Jace's desk. "So, there you go. Let me know what you think."

He slid the papers over to him. "Give me a sec. I'll read this now."

Oh. She hadn't expected that. "Okay. Sure."

It didn't take him long. When he finished, he glanced up. "This is great, Mel. No man-hating verbiage at all."

"Whew," she said with a grin. "Guess I'm learning something." And then, because she wasn't quite ready to leave, she continued with, "I listened to your interviews last night."

"Yeah? What did you think?" Jace leaned forward, every ounce of his attention on her. "Are you a believer yet?"

"No." Maybe? *No.* "But if we have to pick a couple from those we talked with, there are three I like. Geoffrey and Veronica, the couple with the bride deploying and the couple expecting a baby. Even though I think they are far too young."

"Right. Well, we didn't set age limitations," Jace teased. "But if you had to pick just one of them, who would it be? I'm curious if we're on the same wavelength."

She hesitated, thinking it over. "I'd choose Geoffrey and Veronica in a heartbeat if it wasn't for the fact that he couldn't even take a full day off of work for their wedding." Melanie shook her head, feeling the same frustration she had when they'd talked with the couple.

"If I didn't know better, I'd think that statement came from a romantic." Jace's lips twitched in the makings of a grin. "You're sure you haven't become a believer when I wasn't looking?"

She resisted the childish impulse to stick out her tongue.

"If you're going to get married, at least show the day some honor. That's all I meant."

"You have a point, but think about every word that was said." Jace angled his arms across his chest and leaned back in his chair. "Veronica mentioned they'd recently opened their own business. New businesses take a lot of focus to be successful. Perhaps they'd scheduled the wedding for yesterday, and these meetings came up at the last minute."

"Still bothers me," Melanie said, even though she agreed with Jace's take. "But, yeah, I guess they'd be my first choice."

"Good. Mine, too." Jace nodded toward a chair. "You can sit down, you know."

"I have to get back to work, but hey, we're one-third of the way through. That's good news." Even as Melanie spoke, her stomach dipped in disappointment. When the assignment was over, so was her one-on-one time with Jace. Since when had that become a bad thing? "Maybe we'll finish this up quicker than I thought."

"Not so fast, Speedy Gonzalez." Jace twirled his pencil and grinned. "I like Geoffrey and Veronica, but I think we should plan on one more day of interviews at the courthouse before making a final decision. Maybe on Friday."

"Oh." Her disappointment vanished. "Okay, sure. Friday works."

"And I might have a few interviews set for next week. One is with a couple who have been married for fifty-two years. They have five children, *twelve* grandchildren, and, if I'm remembering correctly, a few great-grandchildren, as well."

She blinked, trying to imagine a relationship so solid that it lasted for fifty-plus years. She couldn't. And because she couldn't, she went for sarcasm, saying, "Don't they know about birth control?"

A deep, rolling laugh erupted from Jace's chest. "You

never fail to surprise me, Mel." He stood, rounded the desk and stopped directly in front of her. Their gazes met, and the bones in Melanie's legs seemed to melt.

He brought his fingers to her cheek and lightly brushed them against her skin. Now she lost the ability to breathe. "Um…what are you doing?"

"You have a smudge on your cheek, Mello Yello. Looks like you lost a battle with your pen." His fingers pressed in a little harder. "Nope, not coming off. Think you'll need soap and water for this."

Without thinking, without even realizing what she was doing, Melanie reached up and curled her fingers around Jace's hand. She stepped in closer, lifted her chin and stared right into those delicious eyes of his. "You're making me crazy," she admitted, her voice just this side of husky. "The way you touch me, look at me. Are you playing with me, Jace?"

"You're making *me* crazy," he said. "I…God, Mel, I can't get you out of my head."

"We work together. This would be—"

"Crazy," he said, finishing her sentence for her. "But so what? Let's live crazy. Let me take you to dinner tonight. Just the two of us, somewhere quiet."

"I…I can't." She retreated a few steps. A wash of relief that she had an excuse to say no rippled through her. Because without that excuse, she would've said yes. And then… then, who knew what else she'd end up saying yes to? "I have dinner with my mother tonight. Every Tuesday, like clockwork."

"Ah. Well, maybe another time." Was that regret or relief she heard? "But have fun with your mom. Tell her I said hi."

"Will do." He remained a little too close for Melanie's comfort, so she retreated farther, stopping in his doorway.

"So, um, I'll talk to you later. I should have my intro to show you tomorrow."

Returning to his side of the desk, he said, "I don't want to see it yet. Let's wait until the end, and then we'll go through everything at once." He winked. "Will make the bet more interesting."

Wow. She'd almost forgotten about the bet. Too much on her mind, that was all. "Sounds like a plan."

She turned on her heel to leave. Just as she stepped completely out of his office, she heard him say, "By the way, Mel. You look hot with ink smeared on your cheek."

She didn't respond, just kept walking, but her heart picked up an extra beat. Jace Foster, the man who could have almost any woman he wanted, thought she was hot. With ink on her face, no less. The pleasure stayed with her through washing said ink off, through working on the introduction to the Valentine's Day feature and all the way through the rest of the day.

If her mind whispered for her to be careful, that charming women was second nature to men like Jace, she mostly ignored the warnings. Oh, she didn't intend to act on her attraction—or if she was going to call a spade a spade—her lust. Still, his flattery and attention felt good. So why not enjoy it?

When the workday ended, she walked by Jace's office to say goodbye, only to find the room dark and empty. She shrugged off her disappointment at missing him and headed for the parking garage. Her thoughts went to the night ahead. Hopefully, her mother wasn't planning a surprise get-together with Wade. Melanie would far prefer to be prepared for that meeting.

Reaching her five-year-old Volkswagen Jetta, Melanie unlocked the doors, deposited her purse and laptop on the passenger-side seat and climbed in. A yawn slipped out. Her up-and-down emotions, combined with the events of the past few days, had worn her down. What she needed, she thought as she put her key into the ignition, was an early night. Maybe a long, hot bubble bath first. After dinner with Mom, of course.

She turned the key and...nothing. Not even a hiccup of a noise from the Jetta's engine. Cursing under her breath, she removed the key and tried again. Still nothing. Well, hell. She'd filled the tank that morning, so she knew the car wasn't out of gas.

"Come on. Don't do this to me," she whispered, trying one more time. "I'm still making payments on you. You have to start."

When the car remained silent and unresponsive, Melanie cursed again. Loudly. Grabbing her belongings, she made her way toward the elevator. From past experience, she knew her cell phone couldn't get a signal in the parking garage, which meant to freaking deal with this she needed to return to the office or go stand outside of the garage.

Seeing as it was growing dark, she chose the office. Once there, she called for a tow. They told her they'd be there within the hour. After that, she phoned her mother to tell her that she wouldn't be able to make it for dinner. Oddly, Loretta wasn't upset by the news, claiming fatigue from a long day at the salon.

Then, Melanie returned to her dead-as-a-doornail car and waited.

Two hours later, Melanie parked her rental car next to the curb three houses down from her duplex. Her neighbors, a group of college students, were apparently having a party, because the double-wide driveway she shared with them was full. She was so aggravated about *her* car that she didn't even care.

The shop wouldn't be able to look at the Jetta for a few days, which meant she wouldn't have her car back until sometime next week. Even though her auto insurance gave her a discount on rental cars, she still had to fork out thirty dollars a day for the Ford Focus she'd driven home. She wouldn't be able to afford that for long.

Once inside, she popped a frozen meal into the microwave before changing out of her work clothes into a pair of pajamas. Settling at the kitchen table with her dinner and laptop, Melanie searched for "David Prentiss" to see if she got any hits. She did, but a quick perusal through some of the given links proved that none of them were *her* David Prentiss.

"Now what?" She picked at her dinner and considered her options. If money wasn't an issue, she'd try using another people-finding service to see if she received different information. Or she could run a check on the other names associated with her father's past households. But fifty bucks a shot was a little pricey when she had to deal with unknown car repairs and rental-car fees. So, no, she couldn't go either of those routes at the moment.

She could look up her father's past addresses online, gather information on neighboring houses and then do a reverse address lookup in the hopes of finding a few phone numbers. Maybe someone would know where he went. Or even give her some type of information she didn't currently have. A man couldn't completely disappear, could he?

With that mission in mind, Melanie cleaned up her dinner dishes and left the kitchen. She hadn't turned on any of her living room lights when she came in, so the room held only the soft glow of the outside light pouring in through the windows. A noise on her front porch drew her attention. Probably just some of the partiers from next door, but her stomach jumped when she couldn't remember if she'd locked the door. The unmistakable sound of her screen door squeaking open sent her pulse into overdrive. She propelled herself forward to check the lock, to make sure she was safe. Then, her curiosity getting the better of her, she looked through the peephole and saw…the top of a head. What in the hell was someone doing bent over at her door? She heard rustling, a cough, more rustling.

Suddenly sure she knew what was happening, she flipped the lock and threw open the door, expecting to see her father dropping off another mystery gift.

Her visitor reared back in surprise as the door opened. His jaw dropped, and his eyes grew wide. His hand whipped behind his back, as if he were trying to hide something. Too late—she'd already seen the red-wrapped gift.

Unexpected disappointment hit first, because it wasn't David Prentiss standing on her front porch. Stunned disbelief mixed with…pleasure?…wove in next, because the man bringing her anonymous gifts was none other than Jace Foster.

"Um…Melanie, hey," Jace said, his voice a full pitch higher than normal. "I thought you were at your mom's."

She tried to speak, tried to find anything at all to say, but words evaded her. This was not a scenario she'd expected. Her throat closed tight, and her heart felt as if it were about to explode out of her chest. Her secret admirer was…Jace?

"Why?" she somehow managed to ask.

"Why did I think you were at your mom's? Because you said you had dinner with her tonight." His shoulders lifted in a slight shrug. "And… Well, your car isn't here. I assumed you weren't home."

A million and one questions zipped through Melanie's mind, but she quelled them. For now. Blinking, she tipped her head to the side and pretended she hadn't seen the gift. "Why would you come over if you thought I wasn't home?"

"Well." He coughed and sort of half slid, half shuffled

backward a step. "You know. I…um…just—" Another shrug. "Your car isn't here," he repeated. "I checked."

Humor she probably shouldn't have felt crawled in. She'd never seen Jace this way. He always seemed so in control, so at ease in any situation. Leaning against the doorjamb, she said, "Hmm. Yes. That would be because my car conked out and needed to be towed. That would also be why I'm not at my mom's."

Jace's gaze landed squarely on hers, and concern lit his expression. "Are you okay?"

Nodding, she said, "I'm fine."

A breath expelled from his lungs. "Good. How did you get home?"

"Rented a car." She wagged her head toward the road. "It's the Ford Focus parked down a ways."

"Okay. Good. I mean not about your car, but that you're safe."

"You haven't answered my question. How come you stopped by if you thought I wasn't here?"

His face blanked out, and he dropped his vision to the ground. "I don't know how to answer that," he said in a carefully modulated voice.

She bit her bottom lip, threw caution to the wind and asked, "Was there something you wanted to drop off?"

His Adam's apple moved when he swallowed, but he didn't say anything. Just sort of stood there, body tensed, looking like a man about to run for cover.

"Why don't you come in for a while?" Melanie stepped back but kept the door held open, knowing she was playing with fire but unable to stop herself. "I can make us some coffee. Or if you'd rather, I have a bottle of wine in the fridge."

"I would like that, but—" Still holding his arm behind his

back, Jace retreated to the edge of the steps. "I should probably get going. Sorry if I scared you, Mel."

Oh, no. She wasn't about to let him get away so easily. Deciding it was time to put all of her cards on the table, she said, "Aren't you going to give me my gift first?" Jace's shoulders straightened and firmed. The muscle in his jaw clenched tight and then twitched. "Or is that present you're hiding behind your back not for me?"

"Well, hell," he muttered. "You saw that, huh?"

"I did."

"I can explain." Sighing, he brought the present into view. "I... Yeah, wine sounds good."

"Then come on in." Her tongue burned with the need to ask all of the questions crowding her brain, but she figured she could hold off a few more minutes. Jace eased past her into the living room. She switched on a lamp and nodded toward the sofa. "Make yourself at home. I'll get the wine."

Escaping to the kitchen, she gripped the counter with both hands and willed her heart to settle into a normal rhythm. Even when she thought the presents might be from an actual secret admirer, she'd never once considered Jace. Why was that?

Because... Well, because he'd never hidden his attraction toward her. Just the opposite, in fact. The man didn't have a shy bone in his body. Or she hadn't thought so until now.

So, yeah, this revelation was startling. And, Melanie admitted as she poured them each a glass of wine, brought about a complex mix of emotions she couldn't begin to identify. Flattery was in there, as was wonder and...maybe even a little excitement?

Her disappointment over her father not trying to reconnect lingered as well, but existed in a different compartment. She'd deal with that aspect of her emotions later, but now... Well, now there was a sexy man waiting in her living room.

A man who, over the past week, had surprised her repeatedly by showing her sides of his personality she never would have guessed existed.

And now this.

Before leaving the kitchen, she fluffed her hair and moistened her lips. The fleeting wish that she was wearing something other than pajamas that covered every inch of her body brought a wave of heat to her cheeks. Then, out of nowhere, she heard her mother asking if she'd ever had great sex, and the heat spread through Melanie's limbs like wildfire.

Dear God, she was in major trouble.

One deep breath in, another out, and she returned to the living room. Jace was where she'd left him…sitting on the sofa. His hands gripped the present so tightly that his knuckles were white, and his eyes held a soft vulnerability. As if… as if he was worried *she* would hurt *him*. Impossible. She didn't—couldn't—have the power to cause him pain.

"Here," she said, setting his glass of wine on the coffee table. "You can take off your coat."

"Right." He leaned over to place the gift on the table, stopped, changed direction and set it on the floor between his feet. Melanie pretended she didn't notice his hesitation. After he'd removed his jacket, he gulped down about half of his wine. "I'm guessing you have questions."

"Well, yeah," she said lightly. "This isn't exactly a common occurrence for me."

"It should be," he said, his voice flat and holding no room for argument.

"Well, it isn't."

Jace rubbed the bridge of his nose. "Where to begin?" he said with a sigh. "I guess I'll explain how this started. You will let me explain, right? I don't want you to think I'm crazy or stalking you or anything like that."

"Jace," she said, her voice soft and hopefully reassuring. "I know that."

His chin lowered in a jagged nod. "Okay. Good. So, yeah, here goes. I wanted to get you a Christmas gift, but I was pretty damn sure you wouldn't accept anything I tried to give you. I figured you'd assume I had ulterior motives. That... that you'd think my goal was nothing more than a maneuver to get you to like me, to...ah..."

"Get me in the sack?" she filled in.

"Yes. And damn, you're always so prickly around me. I... just wanted to give you something nice, something I thought you'd enjoy, without any wrong assumptions on your part." He lifted his gaze to meet hers. "The whole idea was my brother's. Grady used to surprise Olivia that way, though she knew the gifts were really from him, but I liked the idea."

"Well, you're not wrong," Melanie said quietly. "I would've thought the worst."

"Right. I figured that," Jace repeated. "So I looked up your address and came by one day when I knew you were still at the office. I thought...hoped...you'd like the doll. And really, Mel, I just wanted to give you a Christmas present. That was it. Or it was supposed to be."

"I love the doll, Jace. She's upstairs in my bedroom, with the other three I own."

His eyebrows shot up. "Only three? I thought you collected antique dolls."

"Not really. I have a few from when I was a kid." She inhaled a mouthful of air, still finding this entire situation mind-boggling. She could almost believe she was asleep, dreaming. "Why did you think I collected them?"

"The Christmas potluck at work. We were sitting at the same table, and...you mentioned the dolls."

She thought back. "I remember the potluck, but I... Oh, wait. Kurt asked me about gift ideas for his daughter, wanted to know what my favorite—" Jace averted his gaze when she broke off to stare at him. "You asked Kurt to do that, didn't you?"

"Well, you sure weren't going to tell me."

One question answered. "And the other gifts?"

A ruddy flush darkened Jace's complexion. "I…ah…see, it's like this, Mel. I haven't gone out of my way to find gifts for you, but I'd be out somewhere and see something and I'd think of you. So, I guess you could say the other gifts happened more by accident than with any purposeful thought." His eyes rounded. "Wait. I didn't mean…I *would* go out of my way to shop for you. Absolutely. It just didn't happen that way, that's all."

"But why *those* books?"

Jace finished off his wine. "I like bookstores, especially stores that carry rare copies. I tend to haunt the local shops, seeing what they just got in. Besides, who doesn't like books?"

Was he purposely avoiding her question? She tried again. "But how did you know which books to buy?"

"It's really not that big of a deal."

She arched an eyebrow and waited.

"All *Gazette* employees fill out a bunch of forms when they're hired. They're supposed to help Kurt figure out who to give certain assignments to, or for any of us to find out if another staff member might have a connection to a story that's unraveling."

She narrowed her eyes and gestured for him to continue.

"It was a great idea that no one has really used, because who wants to pour through a bunch of forms looking for one tiny bit of information? Anyway, those documents are slowly being indexed and entered into our database." Jace closed his eyes for a millisecond. "I sort of dug yours out and entered the information myself. I figured I might learn something I could use to get you to agree to a date."

"Really, Jace?" This should have annoyed her. It would have, not so long ago. For whatever reason, though, his actions didn't really bother her. Maybe because he normally didn't have to put forth so much effort to get a date. It made her feel special. Like he really, really went out of his way to get her attention. She cleared her throat. "So, what did you learn about me?"

"Besides what some of your favorite books are? Um, favorite movies—though you didn't write down how much you like horror flicks. That came as a nice surprise." Jace fidgeted. "Some names of people you've worked with, the college you went to, and… Well, not a lot else." A grin—the first one she'd seen from him all evening—lifted the corners of his mouth. "Contrary woman that you are, you wrote 'not applicable' on more than half the questions."

"Because more than half of them weren't applicable. I don't have any political connections, I don't play sports, I rarely visit clubs or go barhopping and I definitely don't have any interesting hobbies." Melanie wrinkled her nose. "I'm kind of boring."

"You are anything but boring."

"Well…eye of the beholder, I guess."

"I have a discerning eye. I know of what I speak."

Melanie forced a laugh. Her attempt at hiding how strongly his softly spoken words affected her. This—what she was feeling, the strength of those feelings—couldn't be happening. She was just overwhelmed. Tired, maybe.

That was a lie. Hadn't she always known that there was something about this man, about Jace, that flat-out got to her? Yeah, she had. "Maybe you should have your eyes checked, then."

"My eyes are fine, Mel." He hesitated a second, and then,

"I expected you to be angry. I…wouldn't blame you if you were."

"Why? Because you thought of me and brought me gifts? Because you knew me well enough to know that was the only way I'd accept them? No, Jace. I'm not angry."

"But there's something bothering you. What is it?"

"I…guess I'm confused. Not so much about you." Ha. Another lie. "See, I built up this entire story of where—who—the gifts were coming from."

"Who did you think the presents were from?"

She opened her mouth with the full intent of brushing off Jace's question. What she said, though, was, "My father. Because all the gifts were related to my childhood, I grasped on to the idea that he was behind them." The now-familiar heavy weight of emotion pressed against her eyelids. "That he might want to reconcile or something."

The edge of Jace's jaw hardened. "Dammit, Mel. I'm so sorry."

"For what?" she asked softly. "You didn't know about my father then, and you certainly had no idea what I would think."

"But I caused you pain. I… My goal was to make you happy."

"It isn't your fault, Jace. I didn't even begin to think it was my dad until that last gift—*Alice in Wonderland*. My father read to me from that book almost every night."

"Ouch." Jace winced. "I can still be sorry that my actions hurt you."

"I'll be fine." She smiled to add a punch of weight to her statement. "At least now I can stop looking for him."

Jace's eyebrow quirked. "You've been searching for your dad?"

"Sort of. I haven't done a lot, though."

Interest apparently piqued, Jace leaned toward her. "Find anything?"

"A little." She filled him in on what she knew. Strangely, she drew comfort from the conversation. When she finished, she shrugged. "See? Not much to go on."

"Sometimes you don't need much. I, ah, could do some checking for you. What's his first name?"

"David, but no. Don't. I need to think on this. Decide if I still want to move forward." Probably, she would. But the when and how needed to be her call.

Jace looked as if he was going to argue, but didn't. "So... we're okay? At least as good as we were before?"

"We're fine. I'm glad I know, and I...appreciate your kindness." Jeez, that was lame. "We're better than we were before. Though," she teased, "I'm curious about the newest gift."

Jace paled a shade but leaned over to grab the gift, his movements slow and methodical. His focus remained on her, intent and unwavering, as he passed her the present. "This one is different from the others, Mel. I hope you like it."

"I'm sure I will." Doing her best to ignore the fluttery spasms in her stomach, she picked at the tape and removed the wrapping paper. The tiny white envelope stuck to the top of the long, rectangular box snagged her attention.

"There's a card. You've never..." Her voice caught. "There's a card," she repeated.

"You're very observant," Jace replied, his voice steady. Firm.

"Why?"

"It was time."

God, this man confused the hell out her. "Why were you trying to hide this, then? Why were you so set on leaving?"

"I wanted you to know, Mel. But I didn't necessarily want to be here when you found out."

"In case I was angry?"

"Nope. I can deal with your anger, especially if it's deserved." Jace shifted, moving a few inches closer to her. Close enough that she felt the heat of his body, the muscular press of his thigh against hers. "In case I was too chicken to go through with it."

"Oh." Melanie didn't know how to react to that. Didn't know what to say. Choosing the obvious, she said, "I'm going to open this now."

"Go ahead."

She carefully peeled the envelope away from the box and pulled out the card. The front only held an image, that of a bright yellow smiley face. Opening the card, she read the handwritten, solitary sentence, "Consider me in your corner."

Her eyes grew watery in a rush of sappy emotion. "Jace."

"It's the truth, Mel."

She tried to find the right way to express how much this sentiment meant to her. But then, she realized she didn't have to. He knew. It was why he'd written it in the first place. In the end, she settled with "Thank you."

"You haven't seen the actual present yet," he pointed out. "Maybe open that before thanking me."

"I doubt that it's better than this, but okay." Before tucking the card away, she read the sentence one more time. Something hard sort of softened and popped in her chest, and she felt herself take one tiny metaphorical step toward... believing.

"Are you trying to see through the box with your X-ray vision?" Jace teased.

"If I had X-ray vision, you'd be in trouble, buddy." The sexual innuendo slipped out before she could stop herself, but she didn't take it back. Just let it sit in the air between them and focused on the present. She lifted the lid from the box, saw what resided inside, and burst out laughing.

"You like?" Jace asked in humor.

"Well, yeah. Who wouldn't?" She picked up the brightly colored, almost gaudy necklace and laughed again. Red, pink and purple conversation hearts were strung on the stretchy band, each one printed with a Valentine's Day message. She read "Love," "Ever After," "Spice it Up," and "Yum Yum," before saying, "You're a funny man, Mr. Foster."

"I figured all the cool girls need a necklace like this, and you're the coolest of them all. So I had to get it." Jace tugged the necklace out of her hands. "Look at me."

She couldn't *not* look at him, even though she knew to the tips of her toes that what came next could very possibly be her undoing. Not could be, *would* be. Because there wasn't a chance in hell that she was going to turn away.

Not when her entire body craved the feel of his.

So she looked at him, at Jace. His wide mouth curved into a smile. He carefully brushed her hair away from her face. Stretching the necklace taut, he placed it around her neck. "Just as I thought. You look damn good wearing Valentine's Day. Even if you're not a fan, the holiday suits you, Mel."

"Well, the necklace is…charming. I'll give you that." Lightly, almost without consideration, she traced her finger along the strong, firm line of Jace's jaw. Other than his quick intake of breath, he didn't react. "You know which heart is my favorite?"

"Um…no," he said with the slightest of hitches. "Which one?"

"The one that says 'Spice it Up.'"

His body stilled, and unasked questions hovered between them, but he didn't ask them. "That's a good one." He stared at her, his eyes dark and penetrating. Searching. "I rather like 'Yum Yum,' myself."

"Hmm. Yes, yummy things are…good." Now she trailed her fingers up to his temple and then laced them into his hair, waiting for him to kiss her, to touch her. Why wasn't he?

Flustered, she placed her other hand on his knee, squeezed, and waited for him to pounce on her.

He didn't. Okay, either she was really, really bad at this or he simply wasn't interested. Who was she fooling? She sucked at this. Going a different route, she lowered her voice and said, "Your card said to consider you in my corner. You mean that, Jace?"

"Always. That's a promise I intend to keep." He continued to hold himself still, his body tight and restrained. On edge, even.

Well, hell. Here she was, offering herself up, and he wasn't going to make the move. After all of the flirting, all of the sexual innuendo, after everything he'd done to seduce her... he wasn't going to push this moment forward. It was up to her. If she wanted this, she was going to have to go for it.

She'd always been a strong woman. Her head wasn't buried in the clouds or filled with romantic fantasies. And she really didn't care for the idea of having a man in her life 24/7. But she wanted this. She wanted tonight. She wanted Jace. She'd deal with tomorrow when tomorrow came.

Licking her lips, more out of nervousness than anything else, she fluttered her fingers through his hair and tugged his head down, toward her. "What if," she whispered into his ear, "I wanted you in my bed? What would you say then?"

His answer was a low growl in the back of his throat. He lightly grasped her arms, bringing her tight to him. There was a fleeting moment, just a second really, where she wondered if this was a good idea, after all. But then his lips were on hers in a kiss that shattered every cell in her body with its intensity.

Jace arched his head back, putting just enough space between them to ask, "Are you sure?"

Melanie nodded, not trusting herself to speak. Not believing she'd be able to form any words even if she tried.

But Jace wasn't having any of that. "I want this, Mel. But, sweetheart, I need to hear you say it. I need to know that you're thinking rationally and that this is something you really want."

Rationally? What was rational about the fire burning through her, the all-encompassing need to touch him, to taste him? This wasn't rational. This was crazy and like nothing she'd ever experienced before.

So, no. She couldn't claim to be rational. But she did want this, desperately even, so she found her voice and said, "Quit asking questions and take me upstairs. Please, Jace?"

Luckily, that was all he needed to hear.

Chapter Eight

Jace's lips skimmed down Melanie's neck in a tantalizing rush of small, hot kisses. She rolled her head to the side, exposing more neck for him to navigate, giving him more skin to suckle. Good grief, this was heaven and hell all wrapped up together.

She wanted more—so much more—but also wondered how much more she could possibly take.

Myriad sensations thrummed through her body. Each kiss, each touch that Jace bestowed on her, forced her muscles to tense, quiver and then release in a seemingly endless cycle. Her skin literally tingled with pleasure, with a heat that grew hotter and hotter with each passing second. And his scent, that delicious combination of pure male with an edge of spice, surrounded her, excited her and heightened her desire for this...for him...in ways she never could have anticipated. Even the softness of his hair brushing against her feverish skin became nothing short of erotic.

This was Jace. In her bed.

A moan slipped out when his lips reached her earlobe. He stopped there, bit her gently and then wrapped his arms around her and rolled until she was looking up at him instead of down. The weight of him on top of her felt good. Solid and real. His eyes were hooded, darker than she'd ever seen them, and they were looking at her as if *she* were the most beautiful, desirable woman in the world.

She could hardly imagine that was the case, but it made her tremble all that much harder. It made her want him all that much more.

Which shouldn't have been possible.

With steady hands, he slowly unbuttoned her pajama top, his gaze never leaving hers. The intimacy of that was almost more than Melanie could bear, but she kept her eyes wide open, kept them firmly planted on his. If she closed them, she might discover that this was nothing but a dream. And that wouldn't only be a shame, it would be torture to the nth degree.

"Mel," Jace said, his voice deep and husky and seemingly filled with the same need that ravaged her. "Tell me what you like. Tell me what you want me to do." Tossing her one of his devilish smiles, he winked. "Or better yet…show me."

He said the words casually, easily, with the conviction that she'd happily agree. But her building pleasure stilled. Suddenly, she felt strange and self-conscious and not comfortable at all. While she'd had sex before, she'd never taken the lead. The few partners she'd shared her bed with hadn't ever offered, and she'd never felt brave or strong enough to take control.

Now, in this time and in this place, she found she wanted to be brave. Wanted to be strong enough to strip Jace down to nothing and have her way with him. At the same time, the very thought of doing so seemed impossible. And truthfully, she wasn't even sure what "her way" consisted of. All she knew was that she wanted *him*.

The trembles of anticipation changed into vulnerability, into fear that she wouldn't be enough for Jace. That he would compare her to other women and find her lacking.

Swallowing, she slid her gaze to the left of him. "I'm not there yet," she admitted. "I want this, Jace. Please don't doubt that, but I don't think I'm prepared to…to be in charge." When he didn't laugh or pull away, her confidence grew enough that she could face him again. "I guess I'm a little self-conscious. So how about you keep showing me, and maybe next time, I'll show you?"

Her voice wavered there, right at the end, but he didn't seem to notice. His expression never changed, the desire didn't leave his eyes and he continued to unbutton her pajama top without even a moment's hesitation.

"Very happy to comply," he said, freeing the last button. Almost too slowly, he spread her pajama top wide open. Shooting her a look of hunger mixed with pure anticipation, he placed his hands under her hips and pushed up, drawing her torso toward him. Melanie dragged a breath deep into her lungs when his mouth landed on her stomach. His tongue circled and tasted, and her breaths became more ragged.

His mouth moved up, until he reached her breasts and found her nipples. A languid glide of his tongue brought forth a moan; a second slide sent a series of shivers cascading through her body. One breath shuddered out of him and then another as he moved on to her other nipple. Melanie ran her hands along his back, finding the hem of his shirt, and reached underneath. His skin was warm and smooth, his muscles hard and tight.

"Shirt off," she mumbled as she tugged. Lifting his head, he helped her remove the shirt and then returned to his slow exploration of her body. But the sight of him, his washboard-flat stomach and the lean, muscular beauty of his chest, deepened the fire already burning through her until every inch radiated with heat, with longing.

Another long lick, and Jace kissed and caressed his way to the skin just above the waistband of her pajama bottoms. She moaned again and closed her eyes, allowing herself to sink into the moment, into the sensations that Jace ignited with every touch, every kiss. Her senses expanded in a rush of awareness that seemed so much bigger and brighter than anything she'd ever known.

His hands were on her breasts, his thumbs rubbing her nipples in small, breath-stealing circles. Bending her legs at the knees, she tightened her thighs around him and fluttered her fingers into his hair. Never in her life had she felt so alive.

"You are so very beautiful, Melanie," Jace said, his voice rich with his want for her. Moving back up her body, he cupped her cheeks with his hands and brought his lips to hers. He kissed her softly at first, but then with more intensity, more passion. Hell, more everything. Without breaking the kiss, Jace slid his hand down her belly until he reached her waistband, where he dipped his fingers, feeling for her panties.

She gasped when his finger pushed inside, stroking her, feeling for himself the strength of her desire. Tendrils of pleasure snaked up and down her body, pulsated through her blood and caused her muscles to shiver and shake. But it wasn't enough.

Not nearly enough.

Breaking the kiss, Melanie pushed her hips hard against Jace's hand. "You're killing me here, Jace. I think the foreplay portion of our evening should come to a close."

She whimpered when his fingers found a particularly sensitive spot. Giving her the wickedest of grins, Jace said, "Is that so?"

"Mmm-hmm. As in, it should end *now*."

"See? It isn't so tough being in charge." Jace winked, leaned in and gave her another scorching kiss. "Anything else you'd like to say?"

"Condoms. Bathroom. Under the sink," Melanie said in a gasp of mashed together syllables. "And hurry."

He did. When he returned, she'd already removed her pajama bottoms, and she was more than happy to assist him in getting his jeans off, one leg at a time. That act alone ramped up her courage, gave her the bravery she couldn't find earlier. His gaze held hers, steady and sure, while he slid on the condom.

Balancing herself on her knees, Melanie put her hands on Jace's shoulders and pushed until he was flat on his back. She gave him what she hoped was a saucy wink and moved her body into place, straddling him. "I think I rather like being in control. Who would've guessed?"

"I'm not surprised in the least," he said thickly. With that, he gripped her waist with one hand and used the other to pull her to him. Her nipples hardened when they grazed along the firm plane of his chest, and the ball of heat in her belly flared through her limbs, through every cell in her body, when they kissed.

She found the position she wanted—needed, really—guided him there, inhaled a long, deep breath and slowly sank down. Her head reeled back as he entered her, as her body softened and accepted him, and then tightened around him. They moved together as one, her hands clasped in his, their eyes locked on each other. It was a level of intimacy she hadn't known existed: powerful and gentle, decadent and sweet, calm and earth-shattering, all at once.

Shivers danced along her skin, pleasure and need churned in her veins, and as their pace quickened, so did their breaths. Jace let go of her hands and grasped her hips. She pushed down against his thrust, hard. The muscles in her body tensed, held and exploded in a tidal wave of sensations, one after another, growing in strength, until every part of her quivered from exhausted satisfaction.

Jace stilled, caught in that breathtaking second before everything synchronized into being. Melanie watched him, loving what she saw, loving that she could bring him the same pleasure he'd given her. He closed his eyes, and a groan spilled from his throat. His body tensed beneath her for one beat, two beats and then a third, before relaxing in satiated bliss.

Drooping her entire body forward, she rested her weight on his chest and tried to calm her breathing. He cracked one eye open, gave her a lazy, sinful smile and tousled her hair with his hand. "So freaking beautiful," he murmured. "Exquisite."

She didn't argue with him or tease him about having his vision checked. If he saw her that way in this minute, then she'd accept it… Hell, she'd revel in it. "Thank you. You're beautiful, too, Jace. In a manly sort of way, of course."

"Of course." A silent question popped into his expression. He voiced it by asking, "Are you about to send me home?"

"No," she said softly, still stunned by the sheer power of what had just occurred. "You can stay over. I mean, if you want to."

"I wouldn't have asked if I didn't." Tousling her hair again, he said, "Come here, Mel. Let me hold you."

So she crawled off of him and into his waiting arms. They closed around her tightly, securely, as if she was precious and he couldn't bear the thought of her being too far away.

Silly notion, of course. Jace was a smart man. Smart enough to have learned that a woman liked to be held after sex. Smart enough to know that doing so allowed a man to fall asleep faster, probably with less pillow talk. She shouldn't assume that this was anything more than that. Regardless, she wasn't going to overthink a damn thing. She wasn't going to overanalyze, either. Not tonight, anyway.

Right now, her only plan was to spend the night in Jace's arms.

Jace stretched out on his couch to read through his latest draft for "Bachelor on the Loose" and tried to ignore the swirl of nausea attacking his gut. He wished to hell that he hadn't learned about the *Gazette* possibly being sold, because that information was the only thing stopping him from being done with the column once and for all.

But he couldn't let Kurt down. He was more than the boss: he was Jace's mentor. Had been since the summer Jace had interned at the paper, back when he was still in college. Kurt had offered him a job before the internship even ended, on the stipulation of graduation. Jace had been a *Gazette* employee ever since. He owed the guy, simple as that.

Swearing, he saved and closed the file. He'd written about a supposed Friday night out with an innocent-looking vanilla who'd turned out to be anything but innocent. Their fictionalized date included the normal club scene where a local band was playing—Jace had checked to be sure the band actually did play two nights ago—followed up by a nightcap at his "date's" apartment. Where she then proceeded to shock him by wanting to reenact *the* scene between Kim Basinger and Mickey Rourke from *9 1/2 Weeks*.

The article held all of Jace's trademark humor. It had the normal innuendo he had to rely on to toe the invisible line between sexy and raunchy that was necessary for a paper like the *Gazette*. Kurt would love it, as would Jace's audience. Melanie, though… God, he couldn't stand the thought of her reading this and believing it to be true. Especially now. Especially after the amazing night they had shared.

So, okay. He'd push past his stubbornness and tell her the truth before the article was printed. He hoped he'd have built up enough trust by then for her to believe him. He had time. This one wouldn't appear for almost two and a half weeks, and he wasn't quite as concerned about next week's column. After all, when *that* date supposedly took place, he hadn't yet slept with Melanie. Sure, she wouldn't like it any better than those that came before, but she wouldn't believe that he'd left her bed for another woman's. That was essential.

He refused to hurt her that way, refused to let her think that their night together meant so little to him. Not when the opposite was true. Not when he'd never experienced anything like he'd experienced with Melanie. He still didn't know what to make of it, to be honest. The sex itself was fantastic, but that hadn't surprised him. With the physical chemistry between them, he'd known a long time ago that they'd be fantastic together.

But sex with Melanie went beyond the physical. There had been this raw, emotional charge between them that he hadn't expected. He felt it even now, jumping around inside of him like a lightning rod. It scared the hell out of him, because it erased any of the doubts that Melanie might or might not be the woman he wanted. She was that woman. And she now had the power to annihilate him, to crush him beneath her heel and walk away with his heart in shreds.

That was a power no other woman had ever had over Jace.

And damn, she was confusing him. Tuesday night into Wednesday morning, she'd played the part of a woman interested in him. Since then, she'd steered every one of their conversations toward work-related topics. But she also hadn't pushed him away when he'd kissed her after leaving the courthouse on Friday afternoon. So he wasn't quite sure what to think. Still, he worried that she was in cooldown mode, raring up to end things before they barely got started.

His cell rang, interrupting his mental stroll down the worst-case-scenario path. It was his brother. Jace answered with, "Good timing, Grady. I was ten seconds away from bashing my head against the wall."

Grady laughed. "I thought you finished the renovations on the house?"

"Did." Jace had purchased his house as a fixer-upper, and over the past several months had finally fixed up the place. "But that's not what I'm referring to. Anyway, what's up?"

"Couple of things. First, we read the article you sent us," Grady said slowly, "and we talked it over, and we're good with you printing it."

"Olivia, too? I worried about how she'd react." After reviewing the drunk-driving article again, Jace had sent it on to Grady and Olivia. He figured it should be their decision whether Cody appeared in the article or not. "Reading it had to be tough."

"Yup. It was. But we... Hell, Jace, we're both impressed with what you did." Grady's voice lowered and cracked. "Sharing this is difficult, but if it somehow helps even one person avoid the pain we've experienced, then it's worth it. So we want you to go ahead with it."

A knot of emotion closed Jace's throat. He swallowed to push it away. "Thanks, bro," he said, forcing his voice to remain even. "That's originally why I wrote it. But I also wanted to honor Cody and others who...others like him."

"That comes through loud and clear. You'll let us know when it will be printed?"

"I don't know that it will be," Jace cautioned. "Have to run it by Kurt first. But, yeah, if I get the go-ahead, I'll let you know."

"He'll print it. You did a damn fine job, Jace." Grady cleared his throat. "Now, about this Valentine's Day thing. Olivia's all for the idea, and while I'm less inclined to agree, she's managed to talk me into it. So I suppose you can run with that, too."

Jace laughed. His brother was all about the romance but wasn't so fond of broadcasting that he was a softie. "You have to pass Melanie's test first. She hasn't yet agreed to include family members."

Grady's obvious sigh of relief came through the line. "So I still have a shot of getting out of this?"

"That you do. I, ah, was thinking of bringing Melanie to Mom and Dad's one night for dinner."

Grady whistled. "Finally going to introduce her to the family, huh? Mom will be thrilled."

Thrilled was an understatement. Karen Foster would be beside herself over Jace bringing an actual woman home. He'd never done that before. "Think you and Olivia can be there, too?"

"I don't see why not. We're there a couple of times a week as it is. Give me a call when you know the day."

Jace smiled. Plain and simple, his family rocked. "Will do."

Ending the call, Jace stood and stretched. His stomach grumbled, reminding him he hadn't eaten. He put together a quick lunch and returned to the living room. Now that he had Grady and Olivia's approval, he sent the Cody article to Kurt. He hoped that Grady was right, that Kurt would decide to run the piece.

He had just swallowed the last bite of his peanut-butter-and-jelly sandwich when a new email popped into his in-box. It was from Seth. The stress that gathered and grew in-between emails and phone calls from his younger brother eased. For now, Jace knew Seth was fine. Clicking open the email, he started to read and quickly found himself grinning.

It seemed Seth was in the same wacko world that Jace had lived in ever since meeting Melanie. Apparently, his brother had fallen for a local woman sometime during his leave in October. The woman, Rebecca, hadn't replied to any of Seth's recent emails, and when Seth tried to phone her, he discovered her number had been disconnected. Hell, that didn't sound good. Jace stopped grinning and read the rest.

Because he was worried and unable to verify that Rebecca was okay, Seth had wondered if Jace would mind checking on her. It seemed a bit of overkill to Jace. If a woman didn't respond to a man's attentions, that tended to mean she wasn't interested. But if Seth wanted him to pay this Rebecca person a visit, he would. Anything to help his brother stay focused.

Jace typed a quick reply, copied down Rebecca's address and made a mental note to stop by one day after work. He could be wrong. Perhaps there were extenuating circumstances that would explain the non-replies and the disconnected phone. He hoped so, for his brother's sake.

Next, he sent an email to one of his contacts—a private detective that he'd interviewed for the *Gazette* about a missing person's case some time back. He passed along the small amount of information he had on David Prentiss, asked for help in locating him and hit Send before he could change his mind.

Possibly a mistake. He'd gone round and round with himself on this particular subject for the past few days. Melanie had specifically said she needed more time before making a decision. But he had to do something to try to repair the sadness he saw in her eyes.

Besides, he figured there was no harm in getting the ball rolling. That way, assuming his contact was able to find any information, Jace would have it ready for Melanie if and when she wanted it. If she decided to keep the status quo, on the other hand, then Jace just might have to pay a visit to David Prentiss himself.

* * *

Melanie spent the majority of Monday going through the interviews she and Jace had conducted on Friday, noting which couples she thought would work well for the article. Strangely, she had a tough time narrowing down the long list. Instead of focusing on the reasons why a couple wasn't a good fit, she kept latching on to reasons why they *were*.

She blamed herself for that one. Ever since her…encounter with Jace, her head had seemingly become filled with bits of fluff that stopped her from thinking clearly. She'd also developed the irritating habit of daydreaming. About Jace. About that night. About *him* and what he might be thinking, feeling. If that night had stuck with him the way it had with her.

Which then, naturally, led her to obsessing over why she was behaving so out of character. Perhaps she was coming down with a cold. One could hope, anyway.

That evening, she retrieved her car, complete with a new starter. All told, the price tag for the repair came in at just over three hundred dollars. Melanie used her credit card to pay the bill, but that was fine. It could have been worse.

Tuesday, she read through the new influx of letters for her advice column, proofed her current column and got a head start on the following week's. For whatever reason, the appropriate responses to the various relationship questions came to her more easily than normal, almost intuitively. That pleased her, even if she didn't understand why.

Right before leaving for the day, her mother called to cancel dinner, stating she had plans with Wade. When Melanie asked about joining them, Loretta hemmed and hawed with a zillion excuses. Concerned, Melanie pushed. But Loretta assured her that she was fine, that she was busy with wedding preparations and promised they'd get together soon.

Through it all, Melanie did her best to keep a polite distance from Jace. Not because she wasn't interested, but because she was *too* interested. One week of spending time with the man and she'd basically begged him to take her to bed. Worse, she didn't trust herself not to beg him again if they were left alone for very long.

Maybe that wasn't bad. Maybe it could even be good. But she didn't know yet. So until her ability to think coherently returned, alone time with Jace was out of the question.

Whenever he approached her, she was ready with a question about the article, her column or anything else regarding the *Gazette*. She turned down his few invitations to dinner with excuses that he likely saw straight through, but he didn't question her. On Friday, though, he leaned over and kissed her on the courthouse steps.

Hunger roared to life inside of her with the simplicity of flipping a switch. She wrapped her arms around his neck and returned the kiss before her brain could process her body's actions. And then, she spent all weekend wishing she'd turned that kiss into a weekend in bed.

To combat her obvious insanity and approaching meltdown, she insisted on driving herself to Wednesday's interviews. They arrived at the senior-living community at nine, spent thirty minutes with the director and then met with two couples before noon. After a quick lunch, they interviewed another two couples.

Now, Jace and Melanie were sitting in a window-filled kitchen in one of the community's private apartments. This was the interview that Jace had mentioned last week, the one where the couple had been married for over fifty years. Patrick and Doreen Breckenridge were gray-haired, slightly stooped over and in their late seventies. Even so, they appeared healthy and strong.

Mrs. Breckenridge folded her soft, wrinkled hands on the table. "This is so much fun, having you two here. I don't know what we can possibly tell you that's newsworthy, though."

With a wink and a smile, Jace said, "With five children, twelve grandchildren, and—two?—great-grandchildren, I'm guessing you have plenty to share."

A light pink blush stole over the woman's apple-round cheeks. "Well, aren't you a charmer? And, yes, we have two great-grandchildren. Sophia, who just turned three, and Evan, who will be six next month. They were here yesterday," Doreen continued, her eyes softening in recollection. "They visit one afternoon a week."

Patrick set his coffee cup on the small, glass-topped table. "Still isn't enough for my Doreen. She'd have those youngsters here every day if it were possible. Dang ragamuffins, always underfoot. You couldn't walk through this room yesterday, what with Sophia banging on every pot and pan we own. Gave me a headache," he grumbled.

"Listen to the old man." Doreen shook her head in amusement. "You'd never guess he paces by the window watching for their car, would you?"

"Someone has to make sure they don't trample your flowerbeds when they run to the door," Patrick said gruffly as he fidgeted in his chair.

"It's January, dear." Doreen patted her husband's hand. "There's nothing out there to trample. And who was it that sat right here with a wooden spoon in one hand and my soup pot lid in the other, banging away with our great-granddaughter? Oh, yes, that was you. So there is no sense in letting these young people believe you're a grump."

Patrick made a harrumph sound. "I am a grump."

"Yes, dear," Doreen said, her blue eyes sparkling. "Whatever you say."

Jace leaned over the table. "So, I saw an excellent golf

course on our way in. Looked to be eighteen holes. Do either of you play?"

"Oh, you're talking his language now," Doreen said, chuckling. "Why do you think we moved to this community?"

"We moved here because your sister is here," Patrick was quick to say. "But the golf course didn't hurt any," he admitted with a sly grin.

Jace jumped in, asking about Patrick's game. Melanie sat back and watched.

As it turned out, Kurt had been correct: she was learning a lot from Jace. For example, the rhythm to these interviews was vastly different from what they'd done at the courthouse. Rather than getting right to the point, Jace eased into each interview by talking about family, hobbies or life in the community. Then, once everyone was comfortable, he somehow managed to effortlessly change tactics.

About fifteen minutes into the conversation, Jace switched his attention to Doreen, asking, "So, do you have any pictures from your wedding? We'd love to see them."

Again, her cheeks flushed pink. "Really?"

"Why wouldn't he? You were a beautiful bride," Patrick said, no longer playing the grumpy-old-man card. "Go get the photo book, and bring a few from when the kids were growing up, too. I want to show them our house."

"I love it here, but I do miss our home," Doreen said as she left the kitchen.

Patrick looked at Jace. "We started with two rooms and a bathroom. That was it. Every couple of years, we'd add on another room. Took us ten years to finish that house." He nodded toward the space his wife had just vacated. "And her another ten to get her flowers just so."

From there, the interview progressed without a hitch. Melanie and Jace learned how Patrick and Doreen met—she'd originally dated his brother. Only one date, though, Patrick pointed out. Because, obviously, she'd seen the smarter and handsomer brother and fallen instantly in love. Not so long ago, Melanie would've scoffed at that statement.

Now, she wasn't so sure.

The couple shared stories about the early years of their marriage, the struggles they faced with raising a large family and how they'd almost lost the home they'd worked so hard to build when Patrick was out of work for close to two years. Mostly, though, their reminiscing focused on their children, grandchildren and great-grandchildren.

Throughout the conversation, Melanie noticed Doreen shooting speculative glances toward her and Jace, and then looking at her husband with a small, secretive smile. Melanie wondered why, but didn't give it too much thought.

When the interview came to a close, Jace thanked them and started to stand from his chair. Doreen gave him a knowing glance. "I just have to ask...I've been wondering this entire time if you two are a couple. Are you?"

Patrick harrumphed again. "Of course they are. I saw that the second they walked in."

"You be quiet. I'm asking them." Now Doreen rested her questioning gaze on Melanie.

Swallowing, Melanie darted a glance toward Jace, thinking she'd let him answer this one. But he was looking at her with arched eyebrows and that cocky grin she sometimes loved and sometimes hated. Fine. She'd handle this, then. No problem.

"Why do you think we might be a couple?" she asked Doreen.

Doreen lifted her frail shoulders in a shrug. "Oh, it's written all over you. Your body language, the way you both sneak glances at each other and...this might sound silly, but you look as if you belong with each other."

"Body language?" Melanie gurgled. "What body language?"

"I think she means how you keep brushing your leg against mine, Mello Yello," Jace said, a teasing lilt to his voice. "I noticed that, too."

Red-hot heat coursed through Melanie's face. "I…um—"

"And the way you touch her shoulder or her arm every so often, as if to reassure yourself that she's here with you," Doreen said to Jace. "That's how Patrick is with me."

Finding her voice, Melanie said, "That's sweet. Really sweet, actually. But Jace and I are—"

"Dating," Jace filled in without so much as a peek in Melanie's direction. "But we're in the early stages of our…um…. relationship, so your astute appraisal took us off guard."

Doreen's smile widened into one of delight. "Well, isn't that wonderful. I wish both of you the best. You're such a cute couple."

"You're embarrassing them now, Doreen," Patrick said, saving the day. He nodded at Jace. "You'll have to join me on the golf course one of these days."

To Melanie's great relief, the two men launched into another discussion about golf. Smiling faintly at Doreen, she said, "I still can't get over fifty-two years of marriage. Though I suppose after a while everything settles into an easy rhythm."

The corners of Doreen's lips twitched. "I suppose there's some truth to that. But there are days when you wonder if your relationship will make it another week, let alone another year."

"How do you combat that?"

Now Doreen grew serious. "By choosing to stay married every single day. By remembering that we're partners, that we love each other."

Melanie swallowed heavily, thinking of her father. "It can't be that easy."

"I never said it was easy," the older woman said, her voice gentle. "But we're stronger together than we would be apart. A good marriage is worth fighting for."

Jace cleared his throat. "Ready to go, Mel?"

She nodded and stood. Once she and Jace were outside, Melanie narrowed her eyes. "I was *not* pressing my leg against yours."

"You absolutely were. I thought you might scoot over and crawl in my lap. Alas, that wasn't the case. But," Jace said with a sidelong glance as they approached their cars, "I don't recall touching your arm and shoulder repeatedly."

"You did. Like every two minutes." Okay, maybe it was closer to ten. "I kept thinking you were trying to get my attention, but no. You were just manhandling me."

Grasping her shoulders lightly, Jace turned her toward him. "If I didn't have an errand to run for my brother, I would take you home and charm you with my sexy smile. Then I would carry you to bed and show you what I consider manhandling. Based on the other night, I'm guessing you'd enjoy it. I know I would."

Oh! Just, oh! "Well, then I guess it's your loss that you have an errand." How could she want to slap him and kiss him at the same time? "You're impossible."

"Your loss, too." Jace grinned, stepped back and rounded to the driver's side of his car. "By the way, I wasn't trying to pacify the Breckenridges. In my mind, we *are* dating. Which means that you should expect to be wooed. Oh, and we're having dinner with my brother and his wife…Saturday night at six. Are you free?"

"Saturday. Uh-huh," she said weakly. They were *dating?* And he was going to *woo* her?

"Perfect. I'll pick you up around five-thirty."

With that, he donned his sunglasses, waved and drove off. Melanie stood there and stared for a good thirty seconds before her legs felt capable of moving. A pressure she hadn't realized existed lifted off of her shoulders. Well. This was an interesting turn of developments.

Maybe...just maybe, she'd go along for the ride and see where it took her. As long as she remained cautious, what could it hurt?

Chapter Nine

The rest of the week seemed to be attached to wings, flying by so fast that before Melanie realized it, the weekend was upon her. And that meant a date with Jace. She didn't bother pretending she wasn't excited. Nor did she consider their evening a business function, even if the original reason for meeting Grady and Olivia was because of the Valentine's Day feature.

Her eyes darted to her bedroom clock. Five-fifteen. Ack. He'd be here soon. She'd already checked her hair—which she'd chosen to wear loose around her face—and her cosmetics three times in the last fifteen minutes. She'd changed from jeans paired with a sweater to a somewhat revealing dress and back again in the same fifteen-minute span. Now she was strongly considering the dress again. Simple and casual or slightly sexy and feminine?

Dammit. She wished she had more experience with the dating game, but she hadn't been out on a true date for over a year. In fact, the only reason she had the box of condoms in her bathroom was because Tara had given them to her as a gag gift on New Year's Eve.

Hmm. She was really going to have to thank her friend for that.

Melanie had just decided to go for the dress when her phone rang. It was her mother. "Hey, Mom. Are you okay?" she asked as a greeting. "I've left you three messages today."

"Quit being such a worrywart," Loretta said, her tone brisk but not unkind. "I work on Saturdays, and I'm planning a wedding. I called you back as soon as I could."

It had now been over two weeks since Melanie had last seen her mother, which was an odd occurrence—though being happy and engaged probably had a lot to do with that. "Sorry. I'm used to us talking more often, that's all."

Loretta's voice softened. "I know, dear. I've just been busy and trying to keep everything together and moving forward. But I miss you, too. How are you?"

Hmm. Her mother didn't exactly keep it to herself when life wasn't going well. If she claimed to be fine, she probably was. "Good. I have a…date tonight." Wow. Saying that was easier than Melanie expected. "With Jace."

"Oh, darling! That's wonderful! I won't keep you, but I… finally backed Wade into a corner. We'd love to meet you for a late lunch tomorrow."

"You had to back him into a corner to meet his future stepdaughter?" All of Melanie's worries about her mother's fiancé crawled to the surface. "You'd think he'd want to meet me."

"I…was speaking more about his schedule. Why, I've barely seen him this past week, myself. But of course he wants to meet you! Don't be silly, Melanie." Loretta paused for a millisecond, as if to gather her thoughts. Then, "About tomorrow? Say around two. Does that work for you? Oh, and you should bring Jace with you."

"That's fine, and sure...I'll ask Jace." Hey, he was the one who'd declared they were dating. It was completely appropriate to ask him along. "Where at?" After agreeing on a local restaurant, Melanie said, "You're sure everything's okay, Mom? You sound a little off."

The slightest of sighs came through the line. "You need to stop fretting over me. Enjoy yourself tonight, and I'll see you tomorrow."

It wasn't until they hung up that Melanie realized her mother hadn't actually answered the question. Loretta also hadn't quizzed her endlessly on Jace, nor had she buzzed with excitement over wedding plans. Crap. Something *was* wrong.

She almost called her mother back, but decided not to. Loretta probably wouldn't say anything more than she already had. Besides, what if Melanie was wrong? Better to wait until tomorrow, when she'd see Mom in person. And of course, she'd also be meeting Wade. Finally.

For her mom's sake, Melanie really hoped she liked him.

"I assumed we were meeting them at a restaurant," Melanie said as Jace pulled into the driveway of a green-shingled Victorian house not so far from where she lived in Northeast Portland. "Not their home."

Switching off the ignition, Jace said, "This is my parents' house, not Grady and Olivia's."

"What?" Every inch of her skin grew clammy at the realization that she was meeting his parents, his brother and his sister-in-law in one fell swoop. "You should have warned me."

"So you could say no?" Jace turned toward her and shook his head. "Trust me, Mel. My family is awesome, and...I really want them to meet you. They know—" He broke off and shook his head, as if reconsidering whether he should voice his thoughts.

"They know what?" she prodded.

"That I'm crazy about you. My mother would never let me forget it if I introduced you to Grady and Olivia before her. Besides, I've met *your* mother."

And there he went being Mr. Sweet again. Who was the real Jace, anyway? She held back a sigh, knowing she couldn't really fuss. They were already here *and* he hadn't objected to going for lunch with her mother and Wade. Still. "You should have warned me."

"Probably." Skimming his fingers lightly through her hair, he tossed her a boyish grin. "But you'll forgive me, won't you?"

Her stomach flip-flopped. Damn that smile of his, anyway. "Yes."

"That's my girl." He unsnapped her seat belt before leaning over to open her door.

Melanie exited the car and joined Jace on the path that led to the front porch. She pushed her hands into her pockets. "I'm nervous," she admitted. "I haven't ever really done the meet-the-parents thing. Well, once. But that was for my high school prom, and only because my date's parents insisted on taking pictures."

Strong, warm fingers clasped around her wrist. Jace pulled one of her hands out of her pocket and wrapped it in his. "Then you have one on me. I've never brought a woman home. Not even for prom. Believe it or not, Mel, I'm nervous, too."

They were on the porch before his statement processed. "Never?"

"As in zero. Never had a reason to." He twisted the doorknob. "Until now."

"Because of the Valentine's Day article. Right."

"No," he said as he pushed open the front door. "Because

of you. Because we're dating. Because it's important that you meet my family. The article is secondary."

She gaped at him. Of course he would drop that bomb when she didn't have time to process, consider or weigh every word spoken. Let alone decide how she felt about them.

They entered a foyer that had a living room to the left and a staircase to the right. After hanging up their coats, Jace led her to the living room, where he introduced her to his father.

John Foster had the look of a man who'd worked hard his entire life and had enjoyed every minute of it. Tall and broad-shouldered, his bright blue eyes were welcoming as he shook Melanie's hand. That, along with his red flannel shirt and snowy-white hair, brought Santa Claus to mind—albeit a well-groomed and extremely fit variation.

"We're so happy to have you here, Melanie," John said. "We've heard a lot about you."

Melanie raised a questioning brow at Jace. "I hope only good things."

"I suppose," John said with a light grin, "that depends on your definition of *good*."

"Oh, quit teasing the poor girl." A woman entered from the dining room. She had a slender figure, gray-peppered dark blond hair, warm cinnamon eyes and a smile that brought a soft beauty to her face. "You'll have to forgive my husband, Melanie. He likes to keep people on their toes." She stopped in front of her. "I'm Jace's mother, Karen. It's a pleasure to meet you."

"It's nice to meet you, too," Melanie said, trying hard to combat her nervousness. A quiet strength emanated off of Jace's mother, as well as a great deal of curiosity about the girl her son had brought home. "Thank you for having me for dinner."

Before Karen could respond, the front door opened and

two laughing voices trailed in. Grady and Olivia, Melanie presumed.

Jace pulled Olivia into a quick hug the second she emerged from the foyer. When he released her, he asked, "Is my brother taking good care of you and my niece- or nephew-to-be?"

Olivia's wide-set blue eyes beamed with happiness. Placing her hand on her flat stomach, she said, "He is. Though he acts as if the baby will be here tomorrow instead of in August. He's gone a bit overboard on the baby books." She tucked a loose strand of long, dark brown hair behind one ear, saying, "Don't get him started tonight, or you'll learn more about the birthing process than anyone—including me—ever needs to know."

"What? I can't be excited?" Grady asked as he stepped through the archway. "Not a damn thing wrong with being prepared."

John and Karen joined the mix, giving hugs and asking questions. Melanie was too stunned by the resemblance between the Foster brothers to move. Her gaze flipped from Jace to Grady and back again. If she had bumped into Grady on the street somewhere, she would've known in a heartbeat that they shared the same gene pool.

They were close in height and build, had the same hair and eye color, and jeez—their voices were almost carbon copies of one another. There were differences, though. Jace held himself in a relaxed confidence, while Grady's stance was focused and watchful. Grady wore his hair shorter and less shaggy than Jace did, and somehow Jace's features were a tad gentler than his brother's, his jaw a smidge less angled.

While the differences were minimal, and there wasn't a reasonable explanation as to why, she found Jace the more attractive of the two.

Jace, apparently noticing that Melanie hadn't budged,

beckoned for her to join them. Okay. She could do that. They were just people, for crying out loud. Pasting on a smile, she firmed her shoulders and pushed herself forward.

Grady's gaze found her. Smiling broadly, he said, "You must be Melanie. Sorry my dimwit brother didn't introduce us, but I'm Grady and this is Olivia."

"I kind of figured," Melanie said, returning the smile. "And wow. I've never heard anyone refer to Jace as being dim-witted. He's the man-who-can-do-no-wrong at the *Gazette*."

A rumble of laughter erupted from Grady. He gave her a wink. "Before too long, you'll know all of Jace's stories. Then you can blow his cover wide open at work."

"Hey, hey, hey," Jace said, coming to Melanie's side and wrapping his arm around her waist. "Remember I know all of your stories, too. And unlike you, I have a medium in which to share those stories with a much larger audience."

Grady laughed again. "Uh-huh. You do that, bro."

"Is that a dare?" Jace asked good-naturedly. "Because if it is—"

"How old are you two?" Melanie interrupted, loving the back-and-forth between brothers. "Eight? Ten? Because I know two men in their thirties are not about to double dare each other."

Grady and Jace grinned at each other and shrugged. "Nothing wrong with a good double dare," Grady said. "Besides, he's used that same threat for years and has never followed through. Can't say I'm all that worried."

"Is that so?" Jace punched his brother lightly on the shoulder. "But you're not thinking about the Valentine's Day piece that your lovely wife has already agreed to. Who knows what type of interesting tidbits I could drop into that?"

Melanie's lips twitched when Grady sent her a pleading look. "Yeah, but *you're* not thinking that you need Melanie's approval first. That is what you said, right?" Jace narrowed his eyes in mock annoyance and nodded. Angling his arms across his chest, Grady continued, "Seeing as she's sure to side with me, I'm still not worried."

"Oh, for goodness' sake. Melanie's right. You'd never guess that you two are grown men." Karen's firm voice also held a noticeable tinge of amusement at her sons' antics. "Knock it off or there will be no dessert for either of you. Now, though, let's go eat dinner."

Everyone began to drift toward the dining room. Olivia sidled into place next to Melanie, saying, "They go at each other like that all the time, but it's how they show their love." She shrugged. "In truth, they'd do just about anything for each other."

"I caught that," Melanie said. "And I know Jace worries a lot about Seth. Grady probably does, too."

"We all do," Olivia said. "But he'll be home by early June. We're all just counting the days and keeping him in our prayers."

They reached the dining room, and Olivia went to take the seat next to her husband. The center of the table was filled with bowls and platters of food. Pot roast and all the fixings, from what Melanie could tell. Jace stopped next to her, leaned over and kissed the top of her head in full view of the rest of his family. All of a sudden, every eye was on her. On *them*.

Jace didn't seem to notice. It bothered Melanie, though. She'd never been comfortable with public displays of affection, and Jace seemed to thrive on them. Besides which, she'd barely met his family, so a kiss—even one similar to that you'd give a child—flustered her. She sent him a scathing look, hoped he got the message and followed him to the table.

Soon everyone was chattering about one topic or another as they ate. Jace extracted information from Grady and Olivia about their relationship for Melanie's benefit. She knew he really wanted to include them as one of the couples in the feature, and honestly, she no longer objected. Not only did she like Grady and Olivia, but come on, she'd already slept with Jace. Losing the bet now seemed inconsequential to the possibility of losing her heart.

Oh, hell no. She hadn't just thought that, had she?

Yep, she had. She blinked, grabbed her water glass and took a long swallow. Was she really falling for *the* Jace Foster, playboy extraordinaire? Every logical and anal-retentive gene in Melanie's body screamed "No!" but her heart begged to differ.

"You okay, Mello Yello?" Jace asked from her left side. "You look a little pale."

"Yes, fine. Just enjoying this fantastic dinner," she said brightly. "It really is wonderful, Karen. I wish I could cook like this."

Karen beamed at Melanie. "Thank you! I'm glad you're enjoying the meal. Though, if you ask John, he'll tell you I couldn't boil water when we were first married."

"True enough," John piped in. "And I was equally as useless in the kitchen. We ate a lot of cereal and frozen dinners back then." He grinned at the memory. "One day, I came home to find Karen sitting in the kitchen, crying her heart out with a pile of cookbooks surrounding her."

"I found out I was pregnant with Grady that morning," Karen explained.

"And she had it in her head that unless she learned to cook *that day,* she was doomed to being a horrible mother." John leveled his gaze with Karen's, and Melanie knew he was seeing her as he had back then. Young and scared, and probably so very beautiful. "So we learned how to cook together, and by the time Grady came along, no one was starving in this house."

Melanie couldn't stop the rush of gooey, sentimental emotion from sweeping in, nor could she stop herself from saying, "I think that's the most romantic story I've ever heard."

Jace started in surprise next to her, but wisely kept his mouth shut. If he hadn't, she probably would've kicked him in the shin.

"Well, John has never been a flowery, poetic man," Karen said. "But don't let that fool you. This man is a romantic through and through." She nodded at her sons. "He's passed that trait on to our boys. All three of them."

Grady and Jace fidgeted in their chairs at the same instant, which caused everyone else to laugh, including Melanie. She liked this family. A lot, even. And she wouldn't mind having the opportunity to spend more time with them.

Suddenly, the atmosphere grew heavier. So heavy that Melanie could almost feel the weight of the air pressing against her skin.

"Okay, so I heard from Kurt about the drunk-driving article. About Cody's article," Jace said quietly. "He wants me to make a couple of small changes, check a few of my facts, but other than that, he's approved the article to run. It should be in next Monday's edition. I need to know if any of you are having second thoughts." His gaze swept the table, landing on his parents first but stopping on Grady and Olivia. "If so, this is the time to tell me."

Melanie had no idea what article Jace referred to, but she also wasn't about to ask. Not when everyone looked so somber.

Olivia blinked rapidly, as if trying to hold back a sudden onslaught of tears. "I haven't changed my mind, Jace. I meant to thank you right off. The... What you wrote about Cody is beautiful and perfect and... Well, what I mean to say is thank you. Just thank you."

"We all feel the same, son," John said. "We're damn proud. I hope you know that."

Jace coughed to clear his throat. When he spoke, there was a thick quality to his voice that hit Melanie hard. "It was something I had to do. For all of us."

Without knowing why, she reached under the table to grasp his hand, to offer him comfort. He squeezed back. Everyone stayed quiet for a few minutes, then Grady broke the silence by asking Melanie, "Have you seen the article?"

She shook her head. "I'm sorry, but I don't...I don't know what this is about."

"I haven't told her about Cody," Jace said. "I thought everyone should meet first."

Grady nodded, looked at his wife. "You okay if I do this?"

"Yes," she said softly. "Talking about him is good."

So Grady shared a story that broke Melanie's heart into pieces. About his and Olivia's son, Cody, about the tragic car accident three years earlier that had stolen the child's life and how Jace had written an article that was part human-interest, part informational, but that his goal was to "get people to think."

Would this man ever stop surprising her? Somehow, she didn't think so. The real question was whether she was capable of giving what he seemed to want from her.

She didn't know. But maybe she was ready to find out.

Jace watched Melanie fish her keys out of her purse, hoping she'd invite him in but not about to ask. The evening had gone well, and he knew his family adored her. Even now, his mother was probably talking his father's ear off about someday grandbabies and how she'd worried that Jace would never find a woman he'd want to settle down with.

Or maybe not. Maybe his mother had always known it would take a special woman to steal his heart. A sarcastic, quick-witted woman who had no inkling of what she did to him, of the beauty she held. A woman like Melanie.

And she had liked his family. He didn't have to guess on that one; she'd told him straight out during the ride to her place. She'd also agreed to use Grady and Olivia for the article and had suggested they consider using his folks, too. Their story had really gotten to her.

So, yes, the night had been pretty damn perfect.

Melanie unlocked the front door and pushed it open. He watched her back straighten and go rigid before she faced him. Uh-oh. An edge of worry sank into his gut.

She gave him a determined, hell-hath-no-fury type of look. "So, I've been thinking about what you said at the Breckenridges'." Her nostrils flared, showing a hint of her temper. "You cannot simply decree we are dating and make it so. You are not king."

"Whoa there, Mel."

"No." She inhaled a sharp-sounding breath. "You *whoa* and let me speak. I should have said this earlier."

Hell. He'd hoped that tonight might have helped her see him more clearly. Now he had to wonder if she was about to give him the boot.

"We are two people, Jace. *Two.* And that means that I get a fifty-percent vote in anything to do with us. But you seem to keep forgetting that."

Us? Maybe this *wasn't* going where he thought. Smiling, he gestured for her to continue.

"Unless I am somehow mentally or physically incapacitated or I tell you otherwise, you don't get to make decisions for me without my involvement." Putting her hands on her hips, she narrowed her eyes. "Does this make sense to you?"

"Yes," he said, readily admitting she had a point. Even that he might have pushed too hard. But damn, it seemed senseless waiting for her to come around to what he already knew. "I tend to see what I want and go for it," he explained.

"And it isn't as if you're the most forthcoming woman I've ever met. You tend to make me a little crazy."

"The feeling is mutual." She continued to stare at him, as if waiting for him to say more.

He racked his brain, trying to figure out what. Oh. "I'm, ah, sorry for decreeing that we were dating?"

"Are you asking me or telling me?"

"Telling! I'm sorry I played king. Totally sorry."

Her stance softened a minute amount. "Apology accepted. Now—"

"Right. Go on in and lock up." He said the words fast, not wanting to actually hear her telling him to get lost. He'd see her tomorrow. He could—would—fix this then. "I...I can't leave while you're standing outside this time of night."

She blinked. "What?"

Confused, he gave himself a second to consider why she might sound annoyed. But then he got it. She'd just freaking told him to stop making decisions for her, and what did he go and do? Yeah. He told her what to do. Cringing, he backed up a few paces. "I need to know you're safe before I leave. That's all I meant."

Comprehension flickered into being. "Did I ask you to leave?"

"No."

"Then why are you leaving?"

"Because you're, ah, angry with my kinglike attitude?" Whipping his fingers through his hair, he tried, oh, how he tried, to figure out what the hell was happening now.

"I'm not mad, Jace. Just setting some ground rules." She rolled her bottom lip into her mouth. "We can date, but we take this one day at a time. One *step* at a time."

A whoosh of relief, so strong it nearly knocked him on his ass, came over him. "I'm good with steps," he said, going for calm, cool and collected. Inside, though, there was a friggin' band playing and cheerleaders swishing their pom-poms in the air. "Does that mean I'm invited in?"

"For a man who's spent most of his adult life seducing women, you're pretty clueless about females, aren't you?" Before he could respond, she pivoted on her heel and walked inside. Over her shoulder, she said, "Yes, you're invited in. I'm going upstairs to take a long, hot bubble bath. Perhaps you'd like to join me?"

She didn't have to ask him twice.

Chapter Ten

Slightly past eight the next morning, Jace, wearing yesterday's clothes, padded barefoot into Melanie's kitchen to start a pot of coffee. He'd showered, but he'd have to go home for fresh clothing before their lunch date with Loretta and...what was his name? Oh, yes. Wade.

But he decided he'd wait and see if Melanie would join him. He had this notion of showing her his house, of all the work he'd done to the place. But at the moment, the lady was still curled up in bed, fast asleep. Good, he thought as he filled the pot with water. She needed her rest.

They'd kept each other awake long into the night until, somewhere around three, exhaustion had claimed them both. He woke with Melanie's head on his chest, and her hair, soft and fragrant, clouding around him. He held her for a bit, waiting to see if she'd wake. She hadn't, so he figured he'd shower, find his way around her kitchen and bring her breakfast in bed as a small example of the wooing he'd promised her.

Then he'd tell her the truth about "Bachelor on the Loose." He wanted her to know that he wasn't *that* guy, for his sake as much as for hers.

Another thought occurred and he groaned. Based on their conversation last night, he should come clean about the background search he'd instigated on David Prentiss. Jace hadn't heard anything yet, but he'd put in the request over a week ago. It probably wouldn't be too much longer.

How steamed would she be? Anxiety bubbled through his veins. Plenty steamed. The question was, would she forgive him? Would their "take this one step at a time" agreement hold through the storm? Hell if he knew.

His gaze landed on her laptop, which she'd left on the kitchen table, and an idea struck. Going with it, he powered on the computer. Fixing this was simple. All he had to do was send another email to the investigator, this one stating that Jace had changed his mind. If he never received any information about Melanie's father, then he wouldn't necessarily have to share his well-intentioned lapse in judgment.

Okay, a fine line, but an acceptable one as far as Jace was concerned. Or if he did give in to his need-to-share-all complex, then at least Melanie would know he'd listened to her and had acted accordingly. Yeah, either way it went, he'd come out better by stopping the investigation before it got started.

As soon as the laptop was ready to go, Jace pulled up his email provider's website, typed in his username and password, and hit Enter. Scanning his in-box, he expelled a sigh of relief when he didn't see an email from his contact. Awesome. Luck was on his side today. He composed the email quickly and hit Send.

There. Done.

Much more relaxed, Jace poured himself a cup of coffee before sitting down again at the table. Might as well go through his other emails before preparing breakfast. He wasn't much of a cook, but if Melanie had eggs and cheese on hand, he could make a fairly decent cheese omelet. And toast. He could definitely manage toast.

Again, he scanned his inbox, this time looking at each individual email address, rather than simply searching for a specific one. Ah. Seth had written him.

After his impromptu visit with Seth's friend, Rebecca, Jace had informed his brother that the woman was fine and that Seth shouldn't worry. All true, as far as that went. But Jace hadn't mentioned that Rebecca was also pregnant. Well, Jace *thought* she was pregnant, though he couldn't say for sure. But he had to wonder if Seth was the unknowing father or if there was another man in her life that Seth didn't know about.

Regardless, Jace refused to drop that news when his brother couldn't do a damn thing about it. His brother's focus needed to be solid in order to do his job, in order to stay safe. And it wasn't as if Jace knew anything for certain. He didn't. Of course, Jace would tell Seth every last detail once he was stateside again. Until then, he'd keep his mouth shut and try to find ways to unobtrusively check in on Rebecca's well-being.

Clicking open Seth's email, Jace read: "Thanks, bro. Good to know she's fine." He penned a quick reply and was three seconds away from exiting the system when another email dropped into his in-box. A reply from his contact.

Bloody hell.

His investigator friend had been compiling his report on David Prentiss when he received Jace's request. Since he'd already completed the work, he sent the file on. The sick feeling in Jace's stomach returned. He didn't open the attachment, but the email spelled out what he would find when he did: David's home address in Gresham—literally minutes away—phone number and a few other basic facts gleaned from public records.

Okay, so luck wasn't with him today.

Jace logged out of his email and turned off the laptop. Rubbing his hands over his eyes, he tried to work out what words he'd use to explain this to Melanie. He thought back to the day she rushed into his office, her eyes blazing and ears smoking, after learning about the deal he'd made with Kurt. She'd absolutely been steamed. But after a while, she calmed down and listened. The same would happen with this. Probably.

No longer hungry, Jace went to wake his sleeping beauty and give her news that he hoped, when all was said and done, she'd be—if not happy—relieved to have. He hadn't yet made it to the stairs when a knock on the front door altered his direction. Another knock and a long, plaintive peal of the doorbell sounded off before he crossed the few feet to the door.

Opening it, he found Melanie's mother on the other side. Red-rimmed eyes framed in black blobs of runny mascara clued him in on her state of mind. Concerned by what he saw, he ushered her into the house and led her to Melanie's pale-yellow-and-green-striped couch.

Sitting next to her, he took her hand in his. "What happened?" he asked.

"Is m-my daughter h-here?" Loretta's smudged eyelashes fluttered in a series of heavy blinks. "She was r-right, you know. She usually is."

"Right about what?" he asked gently, though he was fairly sure of where this was headed.

"Wade." She blinked again, and two huge teardrops rolled down her cosmetic-smeared cheeks. "M-maybe everything else, too. She doesn't believe in love, you see. Doesn't th-think it's possible to trust your heart to a m-man without being hurt."

"Mom? What's wrong?" Melanie's anxious voice whisked into the room as she nearly tripped head over heels in her rush to get down the stairs.

The sound of her daughter's voice forced a long, emotional shudder through Loretta's body. And then, another wrenching bout of sobs.

"Oh, God, Mom," Melanie said when she got close enough to get a good look at Loretta. Taking the seat on the other side of her, Melanie carefully tucked her mother's hair behind her ear. As if she was the mother and Loretta the child. "I'm here. We can get through anything together, you know that. So tell me, what happened?"

In one of those seconds of pure knowledge people were sometimes gifted with, Jace realized the scene in front of him was one that had played out many, many times between mother and daughter. Probably throughout most of Melanie's life.

"It's over. Already," Loretta whispered. She pulled her left hand free from Jace's grasp and rubbed her bare ring finger. "He…he said I could keep the ring, b-but who wants an engagement ring if there isn't going to be a wedding?"

"You gave him back the ring?" Melanie asked.

"I th-threw it at him and told him to get out." Loretta heaved a breath. "Wh-what am I going to do?"

Melanie gently stroked her mother's hair. "First, you're going to go upstairs and wash your face. While you're doing that, I'll make us some tea. I have chamomile, and that always helps relax you. Then we'll sit right here and you can tell me the whole story."

Loretta nodded and pulled herself to her feet. "Yes. Tea. Tea w-would be good."

Melanie waited for her mother to disappear up the flight

of stairs before focusing on Jace. "I'm sorry, Jace, but I need to be alone with my mother. This... Getting her to some semblance of functional again will take most of the day." Then, with a shake of her caramel-colored hair, she said, "Or longer. This is the worst I've seen her in years."

"Of course, Mel. I understand this is a private moment." He started to reach for her but didn't. There was a glazed-over fogginess in her eyes that bothered him. "How about if I bring us some dinner later? Let me take care of you after you take care of your mother."

"I don't need taking care of," she said, her voice slightly bewildered. "*I'm* not hurting. My mother is."

"Aw, darlin', we all need taking care of every now and then." Giving in, he reached for her and pulled her close. She smelled soft and feminine and flowery. "What is so wrong with a little extra attention after you've had a particularly tough day?"

Her body relaxed and loosened in his embrace. Tightening his hold, he rested his chin in her hair. When she nuzzled his neck with her cheek, he knew he'd won.

"Will you bring Mexican food and really cold beer? Icy cold?" she mumbled. "Oh, and the richest, darkest, most decadent chocolate cake you can find." She sighed, already seemingly exhausted. "I'm always starving at the end of Day One."

"You got it." God. This had happened often enough that they'd established a pattern? That also bothered him. Couldn't Loretta see what this was doing to Melanie?

Well, he was here now. Here to stay, if he had anything to say about it.

Melanie paced a steady path along her living room floor while waiting for Jace to show. Tight darts of pain ping-ponged between her temples, causing her stomach to churn.

This breakup was bad. So bad, she'd insisted that Loretta spend the night at her place. Mom had agreed and was now resting upstairs.

Loretta's string of failed relationships had added to and fined-tuned the coping steps Melanie used to get her through her grief. Chamomile tea was the first step. While sipping and sobbing, the details of whatever had happened would emerge.

After which, Melanie would commiserate by saying everything that Mom needed to hear: "Yes, he acted like a jerk," "No, this is not your fault," "Yes, you absolutely can do better," "I know you thought he might be the one, Mom," and finally, "I'm so sorry."

Anger tended to come next, followed by another round of heart-wrenching sobs. Sometimes, more tea was involved. Other times, one—but not more than two—stiff drinks proved more helpful. Then, with every level of emotion purged from Loretta's body, Melanie would sit behind her on the sofa and brush her hair in long, rhythmic strokes.

This particular step began when Melanie was nine. When she was a teenager, she'd accidentally added another component by comparing an ex from Loretta's past with the most current ex. Obviously, Mom was long over the past boyfriend by then, so the comparison helped her see that she'd get over this heartbreak, as well. Sometimes, a good round of ex-boyfriend bashing would occur. This lent itself to laughter, which was always a plus.

The final steps were a nourishing meal, a hot bubble bath that Melanie would draw and either a movie or TV show if it wasn't too late or Mom wasn't sleepy enough for bed. Without fail, this process had always given her mother whatever she needed to get through the next day, and the next, until the crisis passed and a new relationship began.

This time was different.

This time, Loretta was inconsolable. Instead of giving Melanie the details of the breakup, she'd glossed over them, saying only that "things didn't work out, they never work out." Then, for the first hour or so, she'd repeatedly said that she didn't know what to do, that she'd thought she was finally making the right choice, but that she'd failed again.

Every one of Melanie's coping techniques fell flat. Nothing she said or did seemed to have any effect. And, after that initial rush of emotion, Loretta had become quiet and listless, almost weary. She had an aura of defeat about her that Melanie had only seen once before; the morning after her father's departure.

Perhaps because Loretta's feelings for Wade somehow mirrored how she'd felt about David Prentiss. Or perhaps the cause was simpler than that. Out of all of her mother's relationships, only two men had ever proposed to her: David and Wade. That commonality alone might be enough to trigger similar reactions.

Really, though, Melanie's main concern was helping her mother get through this. But after her epic failure that day, she didn't have a clue as to how to proceed. That scared her.

And God knew she loved her mother. Heck, in every other aspect of her life, Loretta was strong, capable, intelligent and loving. In every other aspect, she'd been an incredible mother—loving and supportive, pushing when necessary and giving her daughter space when called for.

But this…inability of hers to stop making the same mistakes over and over and over had worn Melanie out. This time, she wasn't even sure she *could* help. And the long hours spent trying to do so had rammed in a truth that Melanie had been avoiding.

Yes, she loved her mother, but she refused to *become* her mother.

Maybe Loretta hadn't learned from her mistakes, but Melanie had. She'd just…forgotten those lessons for a while. She remembered now. Would never let herself forget again. Would never allow herself to need a process that included hot tea and a hair brush in order to feel better.

A car door slammed outside, breaking into her thoughts. *Jace.*

Swallowing heavily, she met him at the door. He gave her a brief kiss on her forehead before carrying his armful of bags to the kitchen. The scent of spicy Mexican food wafted behind him, increasing the nausea already roiling in her stomach.

In the kitchen, he was unloading plastic containers onto the counter. Over his shoulder, he said, "I got a little of everything because I wasn't sure what you liked."

"Jace," she said, her voice quiet. Tense.

"I stopped by my folks. When Mom heard you were itching for a chocolate cake, she baked one herself. Said if you like it, she'll give you the recipe."

"Jace," she said again. "We need—"

He turned around and faced her, his brown eyes warm and concerned. "I know, baby. You've had a really rough day, and I want to talk to you about it. I want to know how your mom is doing and what's going on with that. But right now, I think we should relax. Eat. Maybe find a horror movie to chill to. Give yourself a mental break before digging in again."

Oh, God. All of that sounded so, so good. Almost perfect. But… "No, Jace. We…we need to talk. I need to do this before…before—" Before her heart wouldn't let her. Before her stupid emotions overruled her brain. "Before my mother wakes up. She's here, staying the night."

The very air around them stilled as he watched her, as he listened. He shook his head slowly, his gaze intent, his jaw hard. "No, Mel. You're tired. You've had a long day. This is not the time to be making that decision." His eyes blinked shut for a millisecond, and he raked his fingers through his hair. "*Any* decisions."

Now the air grew heavy enough that it hurt to breathe. "I can't do this," she said, her voice broken. "It isn't in me. I thought for a little while that maybe it was, but—"

"It is, Mel. Please trust me on this. I see what we can be. I...*know* what we can be." He held his hands out toward her, beckoning her. "If you'll just step toward me and let me show you, you'll see it, too. I know you will."

The want to do so pressed against her like an invisible force compelling her to move forward, but she shook her head and took a physical step away from the impossible. Away from Jace. "I can't," she repeated, her mother's devastation embedded in her memory. "I won't. I don't have it in me."

"You do," he said stubbornly.

"Don't you get it?" Melanie worked to find words that he would understand. More to the point, that he would accept. So he would leave. Because, dammit, if he stuck around much longer looking at her with those eyes, she didn't know if she'd have the strength to end this. And she needed to end this. That was the only way to be certain she'd never follow in her mother's footsteps. "I can't take the chance. The risk is too great."

"What risk?" Frustration edged his voice.

"What risk? Have you not been paying attention?" Okay, now she was getting mad. That was okay. Anger was better than despair, and she'd take it any day of the week. "Two weeks ago, my mother's life was wonderful. She was desperately in love and excited about her future with Wade. *She* believed that she'd found a man different from all the others. A man who wouldn't hurt her. But guess what, Jace? She. Was. Wrong."

Comprehension dawned. Pain—pain that *she* caused— whisked through his features. "Right. Got it. With no reason at all, you've decided that I'm no better than Wade or, for that matter, any of the other men in your mother's life. That's... nice, Mel. What the hell have I done to deserve that opinion?"

"I just can't take the chance," she said, hating herself for hurting him. "Besides, let's be honest here, Jace. I was never more than a game to you. The one woman who didn't fawn all over you or beg you for attention. In your eyes, I was a challenge. Nothing more."

A mask slammed into place, shielding his emotions. "Do you really believe that?"

She swallowed, ready to push out the lie. Knowing that would be enough to send him on his way, but...she couldn't. Instead, she went with the truth, which really was damning enough. "I did, yes. Now...now I'm not so sure. But I should be sure, don't you think? I should be able to look at you and not have a question or a doubt about your motivations."

"That would be nice," he admitted, his tone almost re-signed. "But I understand that could take some time. I don't mind waiting. I don't mind proving to you one day—one *step*—at a time that you can trust me."

Damn him for throwing her words back in her face. Tired now and craving solitude, she settled her gaze on his. "I don't want to trust you. I don't want to put my faith in anyone but myself. That is the only way I can be one-hundred-percent certain that I won't be let down." She said the words calmly, firmly. Her voice didn't waver or quake. But her heart shud-dered with the loss of what could have been. If she was stron-ger, braver.

If it was in her to take a chance. "I'm sorry, Jace. I really am. But this truly is an 'it's not you, it's me' decision. I need you to accept it."

A long minute, maybe two passed. "I don't know that I can."

"You have to."

He leaned against the counter, as if needing the support, and pushed his thumbs into his jean pockets. "I love you, Melanie. Have from the beginning, I think," he said, almost as if he were talking to himself and not to her, as if he were trying to work out this dilemma she'd presented him with. "So no, I don't think I can accept this. But it's obvious you need some space, so I'll give you that."

He *loved* her?

Shoving himself off the counter, he walked over to her. Using his fingers, he tipped her chin up, so she had no choice but to stare into his eyes. Eyes that beseeched her to change her mind, to give them a chance, to risk it all for…for happiness.

But she couldn't talk. Couldn't even begin to process his declaration.

"I love you," he said again, his voice rich and deep and filled with layer upon layer of emotion. "And I'll wait, Mel. So you do what you need to do. I won't push, but I definitely do not accept your decision. Deal with it."

"Y-you have to," she stammered. "You are not king."

"Nope." Leaning over, he dropped a kiss on her nose. "But you aren't, either." He retreated, giving her space so she could breathe. "Do me a favor and eat the food I brought. Drink a beer and relax. Take care of yourself until you're ready…to let me take care of you."

Then he was gone, and damn if he didn't take her heart with him.

Chapter Eleven

Melanie sipped the coffee that Olivia had served at the beginning of the interview and tried to pay attention to what was being said. Unfortunately, with Jace sitting next to her on Grady and Olivia's couch, that proved impossible. He looked so good, so real, and he was so very close to her. It was all she could do not to scoot over and lay her head on his shoulder, grasp his hand with hers and say, "Okay, you win. Please don't break my heart."

Of course, she couldn't to do that. Because he *would* break her heart. Eventually. She didn't see how a man like Jace would be content to stay with one woman for very long. Or, if a woman existed that could capture his heart forever, she wouldn't be an ordinary woman.

No, she'd be the exception to the rule. Strong. Confident. Exquisite. And, Melanie admitted to herself, the most important trait of them all: courageous. A woman who wouldn't question the gift that Jace was offering or worry about what the future might hold. She'd accept his love, give hers in return and cherish every day they had together.

In other words, a woman who wasn't Melanie.

She stole a sidelong glance at Jace, who was leaning forward, focused on whatever Grady was saying. It had been ten days since the night in her kitchen, when he'd declared his love, when he said he'd wait...that he'd give her the space she needed.

He'd been true to his word. Other than those deep, almost penetrating looks filled with unasked questions, he hadn't pushed, hadn't expressed impatience or frustration. In fact, other than asking Melanie about her mother, he hadn't so much as tiptoed into even a hint of the personal. Most of the time, she was grateful for his control.

Other times, she wished he'd do something, say something, that would prove she hadn't imagined Sunday night. That she hadn't simply dreamed Jace Foster telling her that he loved her.

Crazy, that. Contrary, too, she knew.

But she'd spent every waking minute of the past ten days either at work, working at home or helping her mother process her broken engagement. Melanie couldn't remember a time she'd ever been this exhausted, so if every now and then, especially in those moments before she fell asleep at night, she wished for what she could never have... Well, that could be expected.

At least, that was what she told herself.

Fighting back a yawn, she forced herself to sit up straight and focus on the conversation going on around her. This was their last interview, though they had a few follow-up meetings set for tomorrow and Friday. Then they'd have to get to work on actually finishing the piece.

"For us," Grady was saying, "there was never any doubt that we love each other. It was...understanding that we were different people, that we needed to come to grips with losing Cody in our own separate ways. My process wasn't hers, and hers wasn't mine."

"But you refused to give up," Jace said. "Even when Olivia insisted on divorce. So, from where I'm sitting, that means you had enough faith in your feelings—hell, in *her* feelings— to stick it out. That had to have been difficult, especially with—" he tossed Olivia a teasing grin "—her, ah, stubbornness."

Melanie blinked as Jace's statement hit. Olivia and Grady had almost divorced? They seemed so solid, so...true in their devotion to each other.

Olivia laughed, apparently not offended by Jace's claim. "My stubbornness doesn't even come close to the mule-headedness of the Foster brothers." Her gaze softened and warmed when she looked at her husband. "And thank God for that. If Grady had been any less stubborn, we'd probably be divorced by now. Living separate lives, and we would be miserable."

Asking the first question she had all afternoon, Melanie said, "How did he change your mind? I mean, divorce is a hefty decision. You must have thought it was the right way to go."

A ruddy flush darkened the angled line of Grady's cheeks. "I tricked her. Came here one night and told her I was moving back in until a judge told me I had to move out. When she put up the fuss I knew she would, I offered her a deal."

"Six weeks with no mention of the word *divorce* and four dates," Olivia inserted. "I was...angry. But," she admitted, "intrigued, too. So I agreed. And in those four dates, he reminded me of how—when—we fell in love, of how amazing we were together. Even more important, he taught me that I could think of our son, of Cody, with happiness. That missing him and being sad about our loss didn't mean his memory couldn't bring me joy, as well."

Grady took his wife's hand. "It was rough, and I worried the whole time I was pushing her too hard. But I couldn't not push, either. Not when I believed with everything inside that we are meant to be together."

"Stronger together than apart," Melanie mused, thinking of the words that Doreen Breckenridge had used to describe marriage. Well, not just marriage, she supposed, but relationships in general. "That's beautiful. I'm glad everything worked out. I can't imagine you two not being together, to be honest."

"Thank you, Melanie," Olivia said quietly. "We can't imagine it, either."

Grady started talking about the baby and various names they were considering, depending on if they were having a son or a daughter. Olivia shot down his joking suggestion of "Horatio for a boy or Millicent for a girl." And when Jace suggested his own name for a boy or Jacey for a girl, Grady aimed a throw pillow at his head.

Melanie smiled and pretended to listen, but in reality, her mind was spinning.

Here was a couple who'd survived a tragedy no parent should ever have to face. A horrible twist of fate that could have sent their marriage spiraling into collapse, leaving both of them brokenhearted. Instead, they found a way to bind together, to overcome, and yes—they were definitely stronger together than they would be apart. Not only because of the experiences that tied them together, but because of their… love for each other.

Love that very likely helped them heal in a way nothing else could have. *Love.* That sticky, temperamental emotion that had wreaked havoc in her mother's life, time and time again, was alive and flourishing in this room. In Grady and Olivia.

Love didn't have to be bad. Love could be freaking amazing.

Melanie turned her head to look at Jace. His gaze, steady and sure, met hers. There was want and hope there, like always, lurking in the depths of his dark-chocolate eyes. But she saw something else, something more. She saw…love. The love he felt for her.

Somehow, this moment was so much more powerful than when he'd said the words. Why was that? Why did she feel as if the floor had just dropped out from underneath her?

But then, she knew. With a surety that defied reason, she *knew*. Not only had she become a believer, but she'd managed to do the unthinkable. She'd fallen in love with Jace Foster.

And that realization… Well, it scared her more than anything ever had before.

Jace stared out Grady and Olivia's living room window as Melanie pulled out of the driveway and sped off. Probably heading for her mother's, if he had to guess. From what Melanie had said, Loretta was doing better but not quite back to her normal self. And knowing Mel the way he did, she wouldn't leave her mother's side until Loretta had fully recovered.

Exactly what he'd expect from Melanie, and only one of the reasons why he loved her. God, he wished he knew what she thinking. Feeling. He held on to his hope like a child might a stuffed teddy bear or a security blanket, figuring that she'd tell him again to take a hike if that was what she really wanted. She hadn't, so he hoped.

"She's gone, bro. Staring out that window won't make her come back," Grady said from behind him. "Oh, and Olivia says you're staying for dinner. No arguments."

"Sure. Dinner sounds good." And it would save Jace from another long night of listening for the telephone to ring. Turning around, he said, "Thanks for the interview. It went well."

Grady grinned and dropped onto the sofa. "No problem. Olivia enjoyed herself, and I'm happy when she's happy, so all is good."

Jace sat in the chair across from Grady and rested his head in his hands. "I'm miserable, Grady. Hell, if I'd known that love feels like this…like something chewed me up, spit me back out and then chewed me up again, I'd have run from Melanie the second I met her."

"Nope. You would've done exactly what you've already done," Grady said with assurance. "You're not the type of guy to walk away from anything that's important to you, and seeing how you've been bugging the hell out of me for advice almost from day one, I'd say that woman is mighty important to you."

"Maybe. But this is hell on top of hell with another layer of hell thrown in for good measure. God, the waiting alone is enough to kill a man."

"Then walk away now." Grady spoke as if that were even an option. "Seriously, Jace. You never know what crap life is going to throw your way, so if waiting…simply sitting around on your lazy behind…is akin to 'hell on top of hell,' then walk away now."

"Easier said than done. Do you know what this feels like?" Jace bit his tongue the second the question was out. If anyone would understand how Jace felt, it was his brother.

"Yup. In the words of my idiot younger brother, 'That sucks, bro.' Remember saying that when I told you Olivia asked for the damn divorce?"

"Yeah." Jace sighed. "I was an idiot."

"Yup," Grady said again, with more than a hint of humor in his tone. "However, seeing as I'm partial to idiots, I'll give you some more advice. As I said, you can walk away. Or you can use this time to show Melanie that she won't lose by choosing you. Give her a reason to choose you by living up to your word. Which I believe, based on what you told me, includes—"

"Waiting." Jace groaned. Damn his brother for being right. "You're a jerk."

"Yeah? Well, so are you."

There were flowers sitting on Melanie's front porch. Red roses, to be exact. Judging by how fresh they looked, they couldn't have been left out in the cold February air for very long. Melanie stopped, pivoted and peered down the street, thinking she might see Jace's orange car. Because of course, they had to be from him. But no, not even a glimmer of orange in the distance. Oh, well, what had she thought—that he'd drop off the flowers and then park in the street until she came home to get them?

Maybe. Maybe she even wished he had, because coming to terms with her…feelings for him had put her in a state of numbed limbo. She couldn't move forward, didn't know how or if she even should. Yes, there were couples like the Breckenridges, like Grady and Olivia, and even Geoffrey and Veronica. Couples who were able to beat the odds and forge a life together.

But then she'd look at her mother, at everything Loretta had gone through in the name of love, and fear stopped her cold. Particularly when the man Melanie loved was known for his wild ways, for his ability to charm women with barely a flutter of his sinfully long eyelashes. Not fair, she knew, especially with everything he'd tried to show her, but would she ever really be able to trust him?

So, yes, maybe she wished that he'd push his way into her life again. Make her take the road she was so afraid to travel.

And the flowers, as beautiful as they were and as sweet as the gesture was, wouldn't be enough to propel her into action.

Holding back a sigh, she unlocked her door before picking up the flowers. Their heady fragrance swirled around her as she walked inside. They *were* beautiful. Setting them down on her coffee table, she took off her coat and deposited her belongings on the couch. Then, and only then, did she snatch the tiny card from its plastic holder.

Her traitorous heart did a little dance as she opened the card, as she read the words that Jace had written: "I'm still in your corner, Mel. Always will be. Love, J."

God, this man…he seemed to know her so well. But did she know him?

That was a question she'd asked herself repeatedly, especially over the past few days. They'd spent a lot of time together recently, much of it sequestered in his office going through their notes, talking about the interviews they'd completed, editing each other's work. He hadn't lied back in the beginning, when he said he considered them partners. Every step, every decision on the Valentine's Day feature had been theirs. He trusted her opinion.

Heck, he trusted *her*.

And she wanted to trust him. Sometimes, she even thought she could. But she still couldn't reconcile the man behind "Bachelor on the Loose" with the Jace Foster she'd fallen in love with. Unfortunately, this past Monday's edition of the *Gazette* had served to muddy those waters even more. On the one hand, there was this guy who admitted to his womanizing, player status every other week, in columns that were barely rated PG-13. Often, she actually felt ill reading between the lines…extrapolating what *really* took place based on what he'd actually written.

On the other, there was the man who'd written an article about the aching loss of his nephew, about how Cody's death had affected every nuance of his and his family's life. He'd given statistics on drunk driving, on the number of lives claimed every year, but those were just cut-and-dried facts… or should have been. But no, the article Jace wrote took those numbers and put faces behind them. Put love and life and loss behind them.

How could the same man be the writer of both?

Melanie didn't know. But somehow, she had to find out. Had to prove to herself that she'd fallen in love with the real Jace Foster. And then, well…maybe then she could begin to think about taking the next step.

Maybe.

Chapter Twelve

Jace looked at his desk calendar and fought to keep his growing impatience in check. It had now been nearly three agonizing weeks since that night at Melanie's, and still he waited for her to grasp the fact that they belonged together, that he wasn't going anywhere.

The waiting had only gotten worse to endure. Not that he'd admit that to Grady, who would likely punch him in the arm and tell him to grow a pair. His pair was just fine, thank you very much. And he had no plans of giving up, of turning his back on his love for Melanie or the future he believed they could have.

But optimism was beginning to give way to doubt, and her seeming indifference toward him didn't help. They'd spent endless hours together this past week, finishing the Valentine's Day feature, but not once did she cross the polite-but-friendly line she insisted on adhering to.

To make matters worse, she'd stuck to her love-doesn't-exist mentality throughout the entire piece, only softening her stance the slightest bit at the end. There, she stated that the couples they'd interviewed believed they were in love, and in her opinion, belief was half the battle. But no, she didn't claim to be a believer herself.

When he pointed out that she'd won the bet, he'd expected—at the very least—a teasing smile and a sarcastic retort about how she couldn't wait to see him in a Snuggie. Instead, she'd given him an odd look with soft, almost mushy eyes and shrugged. Shrugged!

Hell, she hadn't even reacted to his "Bachelor on the Loose" column. The day it appeared in the *Gazette,* he'd fully expected she'd read about his supposed antics with the "innocent-appearing vanilla" and roar into his office with temper-flushed cheeks and choice words tumbling out of her luscious mouth. He'd hoped for that to happen, to be honest.

An emotional outburst on her part might push them into a real conversation. Which, in turn, wouldn't only give him the opportunity to come clean about his column without seemingly trying to sway her, but would catapult them into a real conversation.

But she hadn't uttered so much as a peep, so neither had he.

He also needed to give her the report sitting in his top desk drawer, the one on her father. Again, Grady would tell him to man-up and live up to his mistakes, and Jace knew his brother would be right on the money. But he kept chickening out, worried about what her reaction would be. If that would be the final straw in her eyes.

Soon, though, he was going to have to take some sort of action. Tell her about the column, give her the file on her dad, stand under her window at midnight and serenade her…get down on bended knee with a diamond ring. Something. *Any-*

thing to shake her up *and* give him the shot he wanted. But... not yet.

Sighing, Jace stared at his laptop screen, trying to find the will to write another piece of fictional garbage about his nonexistent life in the singles scene. Okay. He could do this. It was his job, after all.

So who was his "date" this time? What flavor should he use? He could go with strawberry. It had been a while since he'd used that one. Yeah, that worked. What did she look like? Was she a blonde? *No.* A brunette, then? *No.*

Somewhere in between, maybe? *Yes.* Shoulder-length, medium-brown hair with caramel highlights and honey-brown eyes. In other words: Melanie Ann Prentiss. Combing his fingers through his hair, Jace swore under his breath. He couldn't describe Melanie as his date, so he tried to bring another woman's face to mind. Any woman. Didn't matter who.

But he couldn't. Didn't even want to. All at once, something clicked inside, and just that fast, he knew the charade was over. Kaput. He was done pretending to be a man he no longer was, a man he would never be again. Even if that meant letting Kurt down. And if Kurt argued... Well, he'd quit. Put in his notice and move on.

The decision felt right. Finally, some type of action he could take *now*.

Jace started to stand, ready to lay it all out for Kurt regardless of the outcome, when Melanie appeared in his doorway. She held a copy of the *Gazette* in her hands and seemed even more hesitant than normal to be near him.

"This is awkward. But I can't... I need to talk to you," she said, her voice low and steady. "Can I come in?"

Jace lowered his jaw into a nod and gestured toward the chairs in front of his desk. A tremor of awareness smacked him in the center of his shoulder blades before traveling down his spine. Was the waiting finally over? "You can always talk to me, Mel," he said. "What's up?"

She sat down and laid the newspaper in front of them. It was folded open to last week's edition of his "Bachelor on the Loose" column. Without saying a word, she pointed to the column and then flipped the pages until she found the Cody article. Oddly enough, both pieces had appeared in the same edition.

"I've read each of these a dozen times," she said slowly, methodically. Almost as if she'd rehearsed these words repeatedly before coming to him. "Possibly more. Now, this is going to sound stupid. What I'm thinking doesn't make a lot of sense. But I can't get this out of my head, so I have to ask."

"You're wondering how I could—" He stopped, gulped for air and prayed that she would believe him. "Sleep with you and then do…go out with another woman. I can explain."

She held up a hand. "Let me talk. Then you can say whatever you have to say."

He nodded even as his gut tightened, even as he waited for the condemning accusations to slip from her mouth. For revulsion to seep into her gaze. What had he been thinking? Waiting for her come to him, to question him on the column was asinine. Hoping for it to happen? Downright idiotic. How could he expect her to believe what he said over what he'd written?

Figuring they were truly at the end now, he sat up straight, steeled himself, and said, "Go ahead. I'm listening."

She gestured toward the Cody piece. "When I read this, the beautiful and powerful words you've written about your nephew, about other families who have gone through the same tragedy as yours, I…recognize you." Her eyelashes fluttered in one blink. Two. A light, almost soundless sigh whispered out of her throat. "I guess what I'm trying to say is that I see you in this, Jace. I see your heart. I hear your voice, feel your feelings. I recognize *you*."

He swallowed. "That was the goal. For people to see...to feel."

Her slender fingers rustled the *Gazette*'s pages, in search of his hated column. When she found it, she shook her head and a tiny frown appeared. "But when I read this, I don't understand how the same man who wrote that touching, powerful article could have authored this. I *don't* recognize this man. I don't see you here at all." Another blink and she lifted her chin, settled her soft, searching gaze on his. "I don't see you in this role. I used to. But that was before we...before I got to know you. And this is the stupid part, but when I read this, I think 'he's putting on a show, playing a part, this isn't him.' But you've written this column for years."

"What, exactly, are you asking, Mel?" He'd heard what she said clear enough, but he wasn't quite there yet. Couldn't quite believe that she saw him. Really saw him. *Knew* him. Maybe...maybe even *believed* in him. "What do you need to know?"

"Am I right?" Without warning, she leaned over and grasped his hand. Her touch, the soft glide of her skin along his, sent a shudder of longing through him. Other than accidental brushes, they hadn't touched since that last kiss, the one he'd given her the night he left her alone in her kitchen. "Which man are you, Jace? You can't... I don't see how you can be both."

"I used to be a man who reveled in the attention of women. I loved the notoriety, Mel. I can't lie and say that I didn't." Oh, hell. What in blazes was he doing? His brain hollered for him to shut up, to answer the questions she'd asked and not give her any other reason to doubt him. But once he started, he couldn't seem to stop. "I was that man for years. For a long time, I thought I would always be that man. So, if you're asking if the same man wrote both of those pieces, then the answer is yes. But…"

"But what? Which man are you now, Jace?" she pushed, her voice neither soft nor hard. Insistent, though. Demanding, even. "Answer me, please."

"I haven't written a true word in that column in over a year. Fiction, all of it." Admitting the truth was akin to the weight of a dozen semitrucks being lifted off of his shoulders. "I haven't been that man for even longer. I'm ashamed to admit I ever was."

"People grow and change. You shouldn't be ashamed of that." Fine lines marred her brow. "A year? I've only been working here since September."

"True."

Dropping his hand, she tapped the offending column. "But you started fictionalizing your…dates before that, before we met. Is that right?"

"I wish I could say that meeting you instigated the change, sweetheart," Jace said, slipping into the term of endearment without thought. "But the truth is, I don't know the cause. I just got tired of it, I guess. Bored, maybe. And I started thinking about settling down, about having a family." He jerked his head toward the column. "And that seemed counterproductive to what I wanted."

And then he'd met Melanie and seen what—*who*—he wanted.

"My instincts were right." Her head dipped in a quick, short nod. "Okay. Thank you for telling me."

"Do you…ah…believe me?" It wasn't as if he had any way of proving the truth to her if she didn't. But he had to know.

"Yes," she said instantly. "I think I knew the truth when I came in here." A small, choked-sounding laugh escaped. "Which doesn't make any sense at all, but yes, Jace. I believe you."

Her belief in him, the fact she hadn't doubted him for even a second, was a gift like none he'd ever received. He felt strong. Invincible. And enormously lucky. Going out on a limb, he said, "I've missed you like crazy, Mel."

"You've seen me almost every day."

"Doesn't mean I haven't missed you."

Aiming her vision toward the ceiling, she sucked in a huge breath. "I've missed you, too. But, Jace…I'm still—"

"That's fine," he said briskly. He couldn't hear her absolute refusal of him again. Not now. She was softening; he knew that. More time wouldn't kill him. "I'll keep waiting."

"I don't expect you to wait," she said as she stood, prepared to leave. "That isn't fair."

"It isn't about fair. It's about you and me. About us." Whoever said patience was a virtue surely hadn't lived through anything like this. "I'll wait," he repeated.

A slow sigh emerged. One of relief or exasperation? Hell if he knew. She nodded and turned to leave.

"Wait, Mel. There's something else you need to know," he said quickly, before he chickened out. "Something I should have given you weeks ago."

Her body stopped midmotion. "What?" she asked.

"Okay, look. You're going to be angry."

She narrowed her eyes, clueing in to his hesitation. Maybe even his dread. "What did you do, Jace?"

He reached into his top drawer and pulled out the file folder, hoping like hell he wasn't signing his death sentence. But if she was going to choose him, if he could be that fortunate, then he couldn't keep hiding this. "Right after you told me about trying to find your dad, I asked one of my contacts to…look into him."

Disbelief and temper colored her cheeks red. Well, he'd expected that, hadn't he? "You did what?" she whispered. "I told you not to. I was specific in that."

"I tried to cancel the request," he said hurriedly. "Right after we had the I-am-not-king speech, but I was too late." Standing, he rounded the desk and offered her the file. "Here. His address is in here."

Her chin trembled as she absorbed that information. "His address? Is in there?"

"Sweetheart, I'll tear this to shreds if you don't want it."

"I stopped looking," she said, her voice now faint and wobbly. "With everything going on…the article, you, my mom…this didn't seem important. But now, now I—"

His concern grew as he watched her struggle. Damn it. Why hadn't he just tossed the file in the trash? "You don't have to take this. There is no law that says you have to move forward, Mel. I can throw this away. You can pretend you never knew it existed."

"But I do know." She grabbed the file and opened it in one fast move. Her eyes scanned the top page, and her cheeks drained of color. "He lives in Gresham? So close. And yet… he never thought about stopping by, seeing how we were?"

"Which is why you should forget about him." Was that good advice? "Or not. You need to decide what's right for you."

"I don't know what's right."

She was silent for a while. Long enough that Jace asked, "Are you okay? Talk to me."

"I wish you hadn't done this."

"I wish I hadn't, either. Hell, if you only knew how much. I'm sorry for overstepping, for putting you through this. I'm sorry for causing you pain."

"Okay. You're sorry." She nodded but didn't lift her eyes from the report. "How can he live so close?"

Jace closed his hand in a tight fist to stop himself from touching her. From invading her physical space at a time she likely didn't need it. "Are you going to go see him?"

Now she looked up. Her eyes were dark and haunted. Distant. "I don't know."

"Do you—" Jace cleared his throat. "Can you forgive me?"

Sighing, she closed the file. "I understand you did this because you care. So, yes, Jace, I'll probably forgive you. Later. But damn it, now I have to figure out what to do about this."

He ached—literally ached—to comfort her. "Can I help?"

"No." The expression on her face clearly said he'd done more than enough in that regard. What she said though, was, "This one is on me."

Then, with another sigh, she stepped out of his office and walked away. And all he could do was watch her leave.

"Over a year, eh?" Kurt plopped his elbows on his desk and frowned. "What about the lemon gal who took you out on her boat and tied you up?"

"Fiction." Jace had waited until the end of the workday before coming to Kurt, wanting to be in his office in case Melanie returned. She hadn't.

"And the snooty rocky road who met you at the door naked with a whip in one hand and a blindfold in the other?"

"Fiction, as well."

Scratching his jaw, Kurt said, "Oh, I got one. What about the—"

"Fiction, Kurt," Jace interrupted, not relishing the thought of going through every last column he'd written over the past year. "All of them are fiction."

"That's disappointing." Kurt gave a tired shake of his head. "Maybe you should consider writing a novel, because if all of that was pure fiction, you've got some undiscovered talent."

"It wasn't that hard. I played the game for long enough that I had...plenty to draw from." Jace cleared his throat. "But it stops now. It has to."

Averting his gaze, Kurt said, "Ending 'Bachelor on the Loose' might not be in the cards. Not now, anyway."

"Then shuffle it in. I'm dead serious here."

"Ain't that easy, Jace. Maybe in a year, we can talk about it." Kurt strummed his fingers on the surface of his desk. "See, it's like this…the *Gazette*'s no longer for sale."

"Well, hell, Kurt. That's good news." And Jace was happy to hear it. "But that has nothing to do with this decision."

"Good news, yes. Except the owners have hired a team of nosy-ass consultants. One of their tasks is to increase our, ah, visibility or some crap like that. They're talking blogs, forums, all sorts of social-networking garbage that makes my head hurt." Kurt returned his focus to Jace. "You and that damn column of yours are the star of their show."

"Then the star quits." Jace spoke quietly but firmly. He knew this would come as a low blow to his boss, but his decision was set. "I hate to do this to you, but I mean it. My life is changing and that column no longer fits with who I am or what I want."

"You can't quit."

"I can." Jace fished the resignation letter he'd prepared out of his jacket pocket and slid it across the desk. "There, it's official. Four weeks' notice is fair, and I'm happy to do that. But I'm done with the column as of now."

Kurt glowered at the folded sheet of paper but didn't reach for it. "You're not quitting."

Knowing this could go on for hours, Jace stood and extended a hand. "You've been an incredible friend and mentor. I respect the hell out of you, Kurt."

"Sit your ass back down in that chair." Kurt pounded on his desk like he was a judge and his fist was a gavel. "Give me a freaking minute to think about this, will ya?"

Jace nodded and returned to his seat, fighting the urge to smile. Quitting wasn't a bluff he'd used as leverage, but damn, he'd far prefer to stay with the *Gazette*. "Take your minute. I don't have to be anywhere."

Kurt slouched back in his chair and closed his eyes. He stayed that way for a good five minutes, maybe longer. Long enough that Jace began to wonder if his boss had somehow managed to doze off. But then he opened one eye. "Do you have any issues with reprinting some of your older columns until I can find a new writer to take over?"

Huh. Jace hadn't considered handing the reins to someone else. It was a good idea, though. A good compromise. "I'm fine with that," he said slowly, "As long as the material is labeled as being reprints."

Kurt opened his other eye. "What about writing a few transition columns to explain to your audience why you're moving on? Say three, maybe four?"

"Two. They can appear in between the reprints and when the new guy—whoever that turns out to be—takes over." The boss started to argue, so Jace offered, "I can maybe write a short lead-in to each of the reprints, as well."

Kurt nodded and sat up straight. "We'll need to come up with something else. Another column." He rubbed his jaw with one hand. "Something that will interest your current audience—or a percentage of them, at least—and keep the owners happy."

"I'm willing to discuss that. Have any ideas?"

"Only one, at the moment. I was thinking about this anyway, before you came in here with your demands," Kurt said, his tone more light than gruff. "You and Melanie worked out okay, doing that Valentine's Day piece, right?"

"Work went well, yes." Jace leaned forward now, curious. "What's the idea?"

"How about if you two keep this up? Pick a topic you disagree on, come up with some type of a bet—silly or serious, I don't care, and run with it?" Sliding his chair to the left,

Kurt grabbed a few sheets of paper he'd clipped together and flipped through them. "Would need a shorter format, and biweekly would be too often. Monthly would work well, I think."

A shared column with Melanie? Jace let the idea sink in, considered what it might mean to work together on a consistent basis, as well as that the focus of the column would be, at the bottom of it all, conflict-based. First, though, he had to ask, "So I take it Melanie's job is safe?"

Kurt appeared surprised. "She didn't tell you?" Jace shook his head. "Yeah, her job is safe. She's managing her column fine, and—" he waved the papers in his hand "—her work on this feature is excellent. I told her yesterday that she's impressed me."

Pride settled around Jace. He knew she could do it. "Good. That's real good. So, about this idea of yours. I like it, but we need to run the whole thing by Melanie first."

Now, Kurt fidgeted. "I already did. She said the same, that we'd have to run it by you. At the time, I was thinking we'd have to drop your 'Man About Town' column, not the other. You're sure you're done with that? Nothing I can say to change your mind?"

"I'm sure. But Melanie likes the idea of this new column?"

Kurt gave him an odd look, one filled with questions. "She does."

Just that fast, Jace's optimism returned. Foolhardy, perhaps. After all, Melanie had already proven her ability to keep work separate from personal. Her willingness to continue to work with Jace really didn't mean a damn thing. Somehow, though, it felt positive. Like a step in the right direction. "If she's good with it, then so am I."

Kurt rubbed his hands together. "Then it looks as if we have a plan I can work with. Maybe you two can even start a blog. That should keep the consultants happy."

"Sure." Jace shrugged. "I suppose we could post updates about the current month's bet and little extras that wouldn't make it in the column."

"Yeah, yeah. That's good." Kurt leveled his gaze with Jace's. "So be sure to take a few photos on your date with Melanie. We'll kick off the blog with the Valentine's Day bet."

Jace felt his brow furrow. "Uh…you mean the Snuggie photos, right? Mel won that bet."

"No, no." Flipping through the papers he still held, Kurt stopped at the last page. "She says right here, 'While I began this assignment with the clear and unwavering conviction that I would never believe in the romantic version of love, I can now state with the same conviction that I am, indeed, a true believer.'"

"Give me that." Jace yanked the pages out of Kurt's grip, found the entry and read it himself. He shook his head and read it again. And then yet again. She was a believer? No. She was a *true* believer. He looked up, saw Kurt watching him with bunched-together eyebrows. "I, ah, she didn't mention she'd changed her conclusion. I thought I lost that bet."

"Well, you damn near gave me a heart attack."

The way *his* heart was jumping around, Jace figured he might be heading down that road any second. *She believed.* "Sorry about that," he mumbled.

Kurt picked up the resignation letter and waved it in the air. "Can we call this nonsense over with?"

"With what we've discussed? Yeah." Today was Friday. Valentine's Day a mere four days away. That was when the feature would appear in the *Gazette,* when Melanie would assume he'd see it for the first time. So…three days to plan his next move.

"One more question and then I gotta run," Kurt said as he ripped the resignation letter in half and tossed it on top of his already overflowing trash can. With a half sad, half hopeful look on his hangdog face, he said, "Earlier in the year, you wrote about a gal who dressed up like Princess Leia, and—"

"Sorry, my man. Fiction," Jace said with a laugh, though his mind buzzed with possibilities. "Complete fiction with a dash of almost-every-man's fantasy thrown in."

Kurt's shoulders slumped and he sighed. "A downright shame, that's what that is."

Chapter Thirteen

Late Saturday afternoon, Melanie tossed her keys in her purse, grabbed the takeout bags of food she'd picked up on the way over and headed into her mother's house. Slowly but surely, Loretta was emerging from her emotional solitude. Another few weeks, maybe a month, and she should be back to normal.

Melanie hoped so, anyway. Once she felt sure Mom had recovered, they were going to have a long overdue conversation. She needed to understand what drove her mother to enter one doomed relationship after another. More important, she needed Mom to understand why that behavior had to stop. For both of their sakes.

She entered the kitchen just in time to hear Loretta say, "That sounds good, Wade."

Wade? What in the hell was Mom doing on the telephone with him? Melanie placed the bags on the counter and went to the table, giving her mother a questioning look.

Loretta offered a faint smile in return. "Yes. Tomorrow at three. I'll see you then." She ended the call and turned toward Melanie, saying, "I thought we agreed you'd go out with Tara tonight. I really am doing better, sweetie."

"Tara had a date. Better, Mom? Really?" Disbelief, shock and no small amount of anger flooded Melanie all at once. "Tell me I didn't hear that you're meeting Wade tomorrow."

"You heard correctly. I am meeting him tomorrow," Mom said evenly. "Why don't you sit down so we can talk about this."

"Sit down? No, I am not going to sit down."

"Melanie Ann," Mom said, her tone now sharp. "Sit down and we'll talk about this."

Fine. She sat down, centered herself by crossing her arms and strove for calmness. "Let me guess. He called to apologize. Probably told you that all the wedding talk sent his fear meter sky-high, but now that's he had time to chill out, he realizes how much he misses you. He's probably asked you for a second—no, make that a *third*—chance. How close am I?"

Her mother's stunned expression seemed to state that Melanie was right on the money.

"Mom, please. Don't do this again," Melanie pleaded. "Don't believe him. This is obviously a man who doesn't know what he wants. And...honestly—" She stopped, shook her head. No, this wasn't the time to get into *that*.

"First of all, it isn't what you think." Loretta closed her eyes for a beat. "I called him, sweetie. I asked *him* for another chance. Because he deserves it. Wade is truly a good, good man, and I am a fool for... Well, for a lot of things."

Mom had asked Wade, the guy who dumped her twice, for another chance? And she was calling *herself* a fool? The same pressure that Melanie always experienced whenever her mother was in a relationship began to build. It crawled into her muscles, tightened them into hard knots and made her stomach churn with acid.

"No," she whispered, her entire body shaking. "Just no. I can't do this anymore, Mom. I love you. I always want to be here to support you, but I cannot watch you do this to yourself again. And—"

"It isn't what you think, Melanie," Loretta interjected.

"And," Melanie repeated, her voice growing stronger, "I can't let you do this to *me* again. I have turned my life upside down waiting for your relationships to crash and burn. I make sure I have chamomile tea in the house all of the time. I keep your favorite bubble bath on hand. When you've been in a relationship for longer than a month, I don't like to leave the house. Just in case something happens and I'm not there to help you."

"Oh, dear." Tears filled Loretta's eyes. "I had no idea. I mean, yes, I knew to a certain extent that I was putting far too much pressure on you. But… Oh, Melanie, I'm so sorry."

Melanie shook her head fast, her own tears flowing, unable to stop the words she'd kept bottled up for so long. "I almost lost my job, Mom. Because I was so sure that any woman writing me for advice must be in a crap relationship. Just like every single relationship I've seen you go through."

Loretta's expression crumpled into devastation. "I've done this to you? I never meant… Didn't see what—"

"And now—" Melanie closed her eyes, thought of Jace and let the tears roll down her cheeks "—now, there is a man who loves me. A man who wants a future with me. A man that I believe is a good, strong, sincere man, and I am too afraid to take the chance. Too afraid to give him my heart after I've seen yours crushed so very often."

"My God, I've…I've ruined your life," Loretta said, every syllable soaked with tears. "I am a horrible mother. Darling girl, open your eyes. Look at me."

"You are not a horrible mother. Not even close. But this… this aspect of our relationship has colored my view on…on men. On love. On what a woman can expect from a man." Now, Melanie opened her eyes. Seeing Loretta's agony, she wrapped both of her hands around her mom's. "You are not a horrible mother," she repeated. "But this…this has to stop."

Loretta gave a jerky nod. "Yes. This has to stop. It never should have gone on for this long. I should have seen what my problems, my insecurities were doing to you. I should've seen that, Melanie." She pushed out a breath. "I know that a child taking care of her mother is wrong, but somehow…I let it continue. Even though I knew better. Can you ever forgive me?"

Dropping her hold, Melanie dried her wet cheeks. Then, she did the same for her mother. "I've thought a lot about this. Listen to me, Mom," she said when Loretta shifted her gaze. "I *know* that what this has become was never your intention. It's only been us two for so long, with only each other to lean on. We fell into a habit that grew worse over the years, until the routine became set. The longer we stuck to it, the harder it was to pull back from. For both of us."

"Oh, baby. Look at you trying to share blame that is all mine." Loretta reached over and stroked Melanie's hair. "You're such an incredible woman, Melanie. Loving and giving, and I'm so proud of you. Do you realize that you have never, not even once in your entire life, let me down? And I am so ashamed for disappointing you. For letting *you* down."

"It isn't so much that. It's… I worry about you." Melanie shook her head as a bit of her prior frustration returned. "Like now. I walk in here, expecting to have a nice dinner with my mother, and I hear you making a date with the guy who just broke your heart. It hurts me when you hurt. So…can you please not see this dork again? Please?"

Loretta sighed. "Honey, Wade isn't the bad guy in this situation. It's me."

"You're going to have to explain that," Melanie said cautiously. "He ended the engagement, correct?"

"Yes. But not until after I broke a promise and not until after he ascertained that I had no intentions on following through with that promise." Loretta's thin shoulders lifted in a shrug. "And he was right to do so. You see, I've had... Well, I guess the best way to say this is that I've had trust issues ever since your father left. I tend to sabotage relationships. Tend to look for trouble where there isn't any trouble to be found. That's what happened with Wade."

"What do you mean?"

Another long sigh. "For this to make sense, I should just start with your father. If that's okay with you?" At Melanie's nod, Loretta said, "I loved him so very much, but you know that. You also know, though we haven't talked about it much, that David and I married because of you. Because you were coming into our lives. But, Melanie, your father never loved me. He liked me well enough, but mostly he did what he thought was his duty."

Melanie had always assumed that was the case, but this was the first her mother had ever admitted it. "Okay. A lot of couples get married because a baby is on the way. I...can see how he might feel that way." And she could, but that didn't stop the hurt from unfurling inside.

"When you were...oh, five or so, I think, he met another woman." Loretta's eyes grew watery again. Melanie hated that, but felt—no, *knew*—this was a story she needed to hear. "And he fell in love with her the same way I loved him. I didn't know about her then, of course. David certainly didn't share that information with me."

"He *cheated* on you?" Why that should come as a surprise,

Melanie didn't know. It shouldn't. Not from a man who later abandoned his family.

"Yes. For two years without my knowledge. I…I'm embarrassed to admit I never even suspected. He didn't behave any differently, didn't stop… Well, we continued to share the same bed. And he was still an attentive father. So I was blindsided when the truth came out."

"How did you find out?"

"The best I can figure is that after two years of sneaking around, the mistress got tired of being a mistress. She gave your father an ultimatum." Inhaling a deep breath, as if to fortify herself, Loretta continued, "Leave us—*both* of us, Melanie—or she was going to find someone else to marry."

Melanie gasped. "How could she expect him to…to leave his child? To leave me?"

Eyes filled with sorrow met hers. Now it was Loretta's turn to grasp Melanie's hand. "I don't know. But David came to me that night, after you were asleep. He wouldn't look at me the entire time he talked, just told me he was done. That he loved someone else so much, he couldn't imagine life without her." Her mother's voice wavered. "Told me he was leaving. Promised to send money when he could, which he did for the first couple of years. And…he left. The next I heard from him was when I received the divorce papers. In those days… Well, if a man didn't care much for visitation rights, the state didn't, either."

Melanie shook her head, denying her mother's words even as she spoke them. Processing this was difficult. She went from feeling sorry for the young mother Loretta had been, to feeling sorry for herself, to being angrier than she ever had before.

"Did he mention me?" she asked her mother. "Tell you to tell me he loved me? Asked you to take good care of me? Anything along those lines?"

Loretta averted her gaze. "Well, I'm sure he knew I'd take good care of you. And maybe he assumed I would—'

"Stop." Bile twisted and turned in Melanie's stomach. "He didn't, did he? He was with me for the first seven years of my life. That night, he left my bedroom after reading to me, came to you and ended your marriage, and then walked out the door without even one mention of me, his daughter. That's correct, isn't it?"

Loretta's shoulders straightened. She tipped her chin to look at Melanie with the fierce light of mother's pride in her eyes. "Your father's actions were cowardly and stupid. Cowardly because he didn't have the courage to stay in your life if he wasn't going to be in mine. Stupid because he lost out on you. And Melanie, if nothing else, that should show you what a stupid, stupid man David Prentiss is."

"This is why you've never told me this story, isn't it? You didn't want me to know that my father didn't love me enough to even ask about me."

"Partly. Also because I didn't want you to think I failed you." Loretta wiped her eyes with the palm of her hand. "Maybe if I had been enough for him, he would've stayed."

"Don't you do that, Mom. Don't you put his failings on yourself."

"I won't if you won't," Loretta replied.

Blinking away the tears that had returned, Melanie nodded. "You have a deal. But now, I…don't want to talk about him anymore." Though, she knew she'd put more thought to this later. For now, though, she smiled encouragingly. "Tell me about Wade. How do you keep sabotaging relationships?"

"Just as I said. I look for trouble where there isn't any. Because of what happened with your father, I only get so far in a relationship before I—" Mom paused, embarrassed, maybe, by what she was about to admit. "I expect problems. I expect a man to lie to me, to cheat on me. Though this hasn't happened with every man I've dated. Some were actually jerks."

"But Wade?" Melanie prodded. "You said you love him."

"I do. Very much. When he ended our relationship the first time, it was because I accused him of sleeping with another woman. I was not very pleasant, Melanie. That scared him, the thought of tying himself to someone who couldn't trust him." Loretta swallowed. "But he realized how much he loved me, so he called. We talked. And when I promised him I'd get counseling, he proposed."

"But you didn't start counseling?" Melanie guessed. "So he ended the engagement."

"Well, there was a little more to it, but that's the basics." Hope glittered in her mother's voice when she said, "He still loves me, though. So we're going to talk. And this time, if he gives me another chance, I won't let him down."

"I hope he does. I hope you get your happily-ever-after, Mom." Standing, Melanie went to her mother and hugged her tight. "I love you lots and lots."

"I love you, too." They separated. Loretta patted the chair next to her. "Now, I want to talk about this brilliant young man who loves you."

So Melanie sat down and told her mother about Jace. How he made her feel. How his eyes crinkled when he laughed. How he looked ridiculously good in a pair of jeans. Even how much she adored his family. Mostly, though, she shared the many different ways that he'd shown her his heart, his love.

By the end, when she'd said all that she could say, the fear that she'd carried around with her for most of her life shifted, changed and...floated away. Part of this sensation was due to her greater understanding of her mother and her father. Of all that had occurred.

The bigger part, though, was so much simpler. So simple, she didn't know why it had taken her so long to grasp on to it. Jace loved her and she loved him. That love was a gift. To let fear—*her* fear—squander that gift into nothingness would be a massive, unbelievable, unthinkable mistake. So, no, she was not about to let that happen.

She and Jace belonged together. Of that, she was finally sure.

Chapter Fourteen

Early Valentine's Day morning, Melanie woke with a jittery, excited feeling flowing through her veins. The feeling was similar to waking up on Christmas morning when she was a child. But if everything panned out as Melanie hoped, today would be way better than any Christmas she'd ever celebrated. Way, way, way better.

Before she started on her preparations for the most excellent day ever, she retrieved the file folder on David Prentiss. The one that Jace had given her. She thought again about what her mother had told her. Maybe she could understand, if not like, her father leaving her mother for a woman he loved more. But leaving her, a seven-year-old child, because the woman he loved had demanded it of him was beyond Melanie's comprehension.

At first, she'd been angry. Now, though, she mostly felt disgust. Mom was right: David Prentiss was a stupid, stupid man, and Melanie didn't need anything from him. Didn't need to look at him, confront him or say one word to him. Simply speaking: he didn't deserve her attention or her time. Not now, not ever.

She tossed the entire file in the garbage. *Now* she could start her day.

After showering and getting dressed, Melanie laid out the three presents she'd purchased for Jace. On the first present— a teeny-tiny bikini that Melanie had only ever worn once— she attached a card that said: "For yard work."

On the card for gift number two—an old-fashioned wind-up clock that she'd snapped off the bit of plastic needed to wind it up, she wrote: "For you to fix." And finally, for the third gift, which was a tin of brownies, she signed the card with: "For your sweet tooth."

She wrapped each present separately in bright red wrapping paper and then put all three in a larger box. At that bottom of the larger box, she'd taped one more card. That envelope read "Open last," but on the inside, she'd put "I'm mad about you, Jace. And I am in your corner. Hopefully, for the rest of my life. Maybe we can talk about that? I'm waiting at home. Love, M."

That last bit had taken her forever to write. She wanted him to know that she was in this one hundred percent. That she was sure enough of him, of her love for him and his love for her, that she'd marry him today if that were possible. That if he still wanted her, she was his. And maybe she hadn't come right out and proposed, but Jace was a smart man.

He'd catch on.

She was positive of that, which was why she'd asked Kurt for the day off. The boss had grumbled but had given it to her easily enough. He'd shocked her when he mentioned that Jace wasn't coming in on Valentine's Day, either. Then Kurt winked at her and told her to have fun.

Maybe he knew something she didn't. Perhaps Jace had

his own surprise in mind, but if so, Melanie had every intention of beating him to the punch.

Once the larger box was wrapped, she hauled it to the car. Her goal was to drop off the present before Jace woke up. Her thinking was he'd step outside to get his morning paper, see the bright red box, open each of the gifts and then show up at her place. At that point, she quit speculating. Whatever happened then, happened.

Wow. Just the thought sent shivers through her entire body.

After double-checking Jace's address—he lived in Northwest Portland—she turned on the radio and sang the entire way there. Had she ever been this content, this excited about what might happen, about what her future could look like?

No. Never.

When she found his street, she slowed down to look for his address. *There.* Jace's house had an angled roof, wide windows and a long, narrow front porch. She drove past, pulling her car alongside the curb a couple of houses down. Her legs trembled when she stood, and her palms were damp when she lifted the present. Approaching his house, she stood straighter, watching his door and his windows, hoping he wouldn't see her coming.

The driveway was empty, but he had a garage. Likely, the Super Sport was tucked safely inside. Adrenaline pumping, Melanie dashed up the porch steps, set the present on top of his newspaper and returned to her car as fast as her legs could carry her. She gave herself a minute to catch her breath. This secret-admirer stuff wasn't so easy.

Tempted though she was to stay, to watch Jace's front door with an eagle eye, she kept to her plan and headed toward home. If he had the day off, when would he wake? How long would she have to wait to hear from him? It didn't matter. She'd be there whenever he showed. What mattered was that she'd finally propelled herself into action.

Her racing pulse calmed the closer she got to home, as did her breathing. Both of which would likely speed up again the second she saw Jace. With a smile on her lips, she slowed her car, pulled into her driveway and parked. Now all she had to do was wait.

It wasn't until she was halfway up her porch stairs that she saw a large, red-wrapped gift sitting on top of *her* newspaper. *Jace.* He'd been here. While she'd been at his place.

Whipping her body around so fast that her vision swam, she searched the street for his bright orange car. Nope. Just like with the flowers, not a glimmer in sight.

She didn't know if she should laugh or cry. Who would've guessed they'd have the same plan for the same day? And she thought she was being so clever.

Picking up the present, she weighed it in her hands. It was a medium-size box, but rather light, and she didn't see a card. Though maybe he'd done the same as she and put the card inside the box. Pleasure soaked in as she wondered what he might have chosen for her.

Melanie stood there, staring at the box, unsure of what to do. Should she open the gift now or wait for Jace? Maybe she should go back to his place to see if she could catch him there. Or…perhaps she should sit her butt down on the porch steps, stare longingly at the street and jump up and down for joy the very second she saw his orange car.

Yes. She liked that plan the most. Besides, that trembling, shivering, sweaty-palm, crazy-pulse thing was happening to her again. She probably shouldn't drive under those conditions. Keeping the gift in her arms, Melanie sat down on the top porch step and craned her neck in the direction she figured Jace would drive in. And then, she waited.

Chilly winds froze her cheeks within minutes, but she didn't care. After a while, her bottom numbed as the cold seeped in through her clothes. Again, she didn't care. She didn't move, either. Not to go inside where she could wait in warmth and comfort, not to her car where she'd have almost the same vantage point but would be out of the wind.

She *couldn't* move. Not until she saw the man she loved.

Her eyes began to water, a result of the wind and the cold, and probably also from the emotion zipping through her with such ferocity. That was okay. She'd wait here, just as he'd waited for her all of those weeks. Well, she wouldn't be able to sit here for weeks. Or heck, even another thirty minutes. But for now, she liked the symbolism.

Another ten minutes or so passed when a new thought occurred. What if...oh, Dear God. What if, at this very moment, he was waiting for her on *his* porch?

Thankfully, that thought had barely processed when she saw a blur of bright orange several blocks in the distance. A blur of bright orange that was coming her way. She decided at that second that orange, especially that shade of orange, was her new favorite color. She might go out and buy an entire new wardrobe in that color.

His car got closer and closer. Soon enough, she could even see the shaggy cut of his dark hair through his windshield. And then, there he was, parking the car in front of her house. Walking—no, striding—up the sidewalk, up the walkway, up the stairs...to her.

"Jace," she said, her voice much more a whisper than anything else. "I've been waiting for you. Sitting right here."

And then he smiled, and her heart melted and her toes tingled—though perhaps that was another side effect from the cold—and her entire body went weightless. If her thighs weren't frozen to the porch, she might have even floated away.

"Hi, there," Jace said, his eyes so dark they were almost black. "I was waiting, too. For a while, but then I got impatient. You didn't answer your cell."

"Inside," she murmured. "Didn't think I'd be out for long."

"Ah." He set his present down, crouched in front of her, and touched her cheek. "Hey," he said softly, "You're freezing. Let's go in. We can open our gifts there."

"Okay, but you might have to help me up. I'm sort of frozen." She smiled. Brightly, broadly. "It's Valentine's Day, Jace."

"Happy St. Valentine's Day, Mel," Jace said, his voice warm and husky, soft and sensual. God, the man had an excellent voice. The sound of it made her tingle all that much more. "Let's get you inside. You really look cold."

They went in, deposited their individual presents on the coffee table and sat next to each other on the sofa. His thigh pressed against hers, and the warmth of him radiated into her. Again, the feeling of Christmas-morning joy came over her. But it wasn't Christmas. Heck, maybe after today, St. Valentine's Day would be her favorite holiday.

She liked that thought, too.

"How did you know I'd be here?" she asked. "Did Kurt tell you I'd used a vacation day?"

"No. I just assumed you'd be home." Jace reached over and lightly pushed her hair out of her eyes. "I'm glad I assumed right."

"Me, too." Melanie cleared her throat. "So, presents. I'd like you to open mine first. If you don't mind."

But Jace was already shaking his head. "No dice, Mel. You have to go first." He picked up the gift and set it on her lap, as if to say he wouldn't take no for an answer. "I thought about this one for a while. I hope you…I hope you like it."

Impatient for him to get to her presents, she ripped the paper off as if it truly were Christmas morning. Lifting the lid, she blinked. Then, she touched the soft, blue, folded-up square of thick, fuzzy fabric. "A blanket?" she asked. Okay. So maybe this wasn't the most romantic gift she'd ever received, but still. Jace had given it to her. That was romantic enough.

"Pick it up, Mel," he said thickly. "It isn't a blanket."

Melanie nodded and lifted the material out of the box with a flip. The soft fabric unfolded and spread across the top of her legs. "It's a Snuggie? You bought me a Snuggie?"

"Not just any Snuggie." His mouth split into a wide grin at her look of bewilderment. "A special Snuggie."

"There are special Snuggies?" she asked, working to keep a straight face.

"There are." He reached over to pull and tug and straighten until the Snuggie was out flat. "Look, it's a Snuggie made for two. Even has three sleeves, Mel," he said, as if the entire idea tickled him to no end.

Melanie laughed at his look of delight. She couldn't help it.

"I thought, hoped, that you'd give me good news today. So I thought…and hoped…that maybe we could have a picture of us taken in this to use for our new column." Then he gave her a sweet, almost bashful smile. "If you'll have me, that is."

"I love the Snuggie, Jace. I love the sentiment behind it, too." God, she could hardly stand the wait. She wanted to shout out that she loved him with every cell in her body. But… "Open my present. I think that will answer your question."

So he did. Following her lead, he tore the paper off in huge strips. When he saw the three wrapped gifts nestled inside the larger box, his forehead creased. "Does it matter which order I open them?"

She shook her head no, leaned forward and waited with bated breath. This was going to kill her. No doubt about it.

The bikini came first. His jaw worked as he stared at the

flimsy straps of fabric in confusion. "Um, Mel. I don't think this will fit me, and I'm not really into—"

"Read the card," she said, pressing her lips together tightly to stop herself from laughing. Because he was too damn slow, she plucked the card out of his hand. "Never mind, I'll read it for you. It says, 'For yard work.'"

His gaze switched from the bikini to the card and back again. Comprehension sifted over him. "Veronica and Geoffrey. This is your way of telling me…"

"That you have two more presents to open," she teased. "So get to it, boy."

"Boy? I'll have you know—"

Melanie tossed another present at him. This one turned out to be the brownies. He read the card this time, and the air between them crackled with heat. With electricity.

"Maybe I'll feed these to you later." His voice held the hint of a promise she intended to make him keep.

But all she said was, "Go on. There's one more present."

He opened the third gift—the clock—quickly. He waggled one brow, saying, "Sorry, babe. This isn't repairable. Guess you'll have to find another way to wake up in the morning. I'm an early riser. So, if you're looking for volunteers…"

Melanie lunged for the last card before Jace even saw it. Nerves tumbled through her, and her mouth went dry. Would he know what she was getting at? If he did, would he say yes?

"This one, I want to read to you." The second she spoke, she knew she couldn't. Wasn't quite that brave. Not yet, anyway. Thrusting the card toward him, she said, "Actually, no. You read it, but to yourself."

Jace regarded her quizzically, but didn't argue. Strong fingers pulled the card out of the envelope. She held herself still, barely able to breathe, and watched him carefully as he read. All the while, she tried to pretend she wasn't about to crawl out of her skin.

Almost in slow motion, a series of minuscule events happened that Melanie would remember for the rest of her life. For longer, if possible.

First, Jace's jaw hardened and firmed. Then his shoulders did the same. Muscle by muscle, his entire body went rock-solid, and his chest stopped moving as he seemingly held his breath. So very slowly, his jaw jerked up until their gazes met. One long whoosh of air escaped from his lungs.

"Melanie," he said, his tone deep and serious.

"Jace," she said, pulling together every scrap of her courage. "I love you. So much. More than I ever thought possible. And I believe in you. I trust you. And I want to know if—"

"Stop," he said, his voice now brusque. "Stop."

Oh, God. "But…" She wouldn't beg, and she damn well refused to cry. So he didn't want to accept her proposal, so what? He loved her, she *knew* that. Besides, she'd known this was a risk going in. More time would be good…smart, even. "We'll go back to the dating thing. That's fine! I—" She narrowed her eyes as Jace suddenly got down on one knee. "What are you doing?"

He reached behind him, searching for and finding the coat he'd shrugged off earlier. "Shh, Mel. Give me a second here."

A million and one shivers hit her all at once. Her teeth started chattering, and goose bumps coated her skin. She wasn't even cold, for goodness' sake. Rubbing her arms, she said, "Seriously, Jace. What are you doing?"

Bringing his hand back into view, he gave her the smile that she sometimes loved, sometimes hated. Today, she thought she loved it. He held out a small velvet box. Instantly, her breath locked in her lungs. Instantly, time stopped. On the heels of that, she stopped *him*.

"Oh, no," she said quickly, before he could push the words out that *she'd* intended to say. "Huh-uh! I was going to propose to you. So…*you* stop."

With a wink and a grin, Jace said, "I have the ring. You have a card. Diamond trumps paper any day of the week, so I say I win this battle."

"Unfair," she pointed out. "Men don't wear engagement rings. Otherwise, I'd have bought you the biggest diamond you've ever seen." Um. "That I can afford."

"Melanie," Jace said, undeterred. "I love you with all of my heart. When I look at you, my heart sings. Why, the day you walked into my life, I—"

"Jace, you make me believe in forever!" Melanie leaned forward and stared into his eyes. "You make me believe in happily-ever-after. When I see you—"

"You stunned me the second I saw you. I knew right off that my life—"

They stopped and stared at each other for ten seconds, maybe twenty.

"Will you marry me?" they both said in pretty much perfect unison.

Silence surrounded them. Jace reached over to clasp her left hand. "I asked first," he said, sliding the ring onto her finger.

She held her hand up to see the ring. "This is so beautiful, but no. You're wrong. I asked first. Like an entire millisecond before you."

Jace shook his head in amusement. "Must you always be so contrary?"

"You're the stubborn one," Melanie said with conviction. "I had this entire scene planned out, from beginning to end. And you interrupted me."

Standing, Jace reached over to pull her to her feet. He lifted her into his arms, saying, "What? You think I had an engagement ring in my pocket by accident?"

She sighed and rested her head against his chest. She felt

safe, cherished and so very, very loved. Not to mention, extraordinarily lucky.

"I know," she said, wrapping her arms around Jace's neck. "How about if you just shut up and kiss me?"

And so he did.

* * * * *

HEART & HOME

Heartwarming romances where love can
happen right when you least expect it.

You can find more information on upcoming Harlequin® titles,
free excerpts and more at www.HarlequinInsideRomance.com.

HSECNM0212

REQUEST YOUR FREE BOOKS!

2 FREE NOVELS PLUS 2 FREE GIFTS!

 Harlequin®

SPECIAL EDITION

Life, Love & Family

YES! Please send me 2 FREE Harlequin® Special Edition novels and my 2 FREE gifts (gifts are worth about $10). After receiving them, if I don't wish to receive any more books, I can return the shipping statement marked "cancel." If I don't cancel, I will receive 6 brand-new novels every month and be billed just $4.49 per book in the U.S. or $5.24 per book in Canada. That's a saving of at least 14% off the cover price! It's quite a bargain! Shipping and handling is just 50¢ per book in the U.S. and 75¢ per book in Canada.* I understand that accepting the 2 free books and gifts places me under no obligation to buy anything. I can always return a shipment and cancel at any time. Even if I never buy another book, the two free books and gifts are mine to keep forever.

235/335 HDN FEGF

Name	(PLEASE PRINT)

Address	Apt. #

City	State/Prov.	Zip/Postal Code

Signature (if under 18, a parent or guardian must sign)

Mail to the **Reader Service:**
IN U.S.A.: P.O. Box 1867, Buffalo, NY 14240-1867
IN CANADA: P.O. Box 609, Fort Erie, Ontario L2A 5X3

Not valid for current subscribers to Harlequin Special Edition books.

Want to try two free books from another line?
Call 1-800-873-8635 or visit www.ReaderService.com.

* Terms and prices subject to change without notice. Prices do not include applicable taxes. Sales tax applicable in N.Y. Canadian residents will be charged applicable taxes. Offer not valid in Quebec. This offer is limited to one order per household. All orders subject to credit approval. Credit or debit balances in a customer's account(s) may be offset by any other outstanding balance owed by or to the customer. Please allow 4 to 6 weeks for delivery. Offer available while quantities last.

Your Privacy—The Reader Service is committed to protecting your privacy. Our Privacy Policy is available online at www.ReaderService.com or upon request from the Reader Service.

We make a portion of our mailing list available to reputable third parties that offer products we believe may interest you. If you prefer that we not exchange your name with third parties, or if you wish to clarify or modify your communication preferences, please visit us at www.ReaderService.com/consumerchoice or write to us at Reader Service Preference Service, P.O. Box 9062, Buffalo, NY 14269. Include your complete name and address.

Get swept away with author

CATHY GILLEN THACKER

and her new miniseries

Legends of Laramie County

On the Cartwright ranch, it's the women
who endure and run the ranch—and it's time for
lawyer Liz Cartwright to take over. Needing some help
around the ranch, Liz hires Travis Anderson, a fellow
attorney, and Liz's high-school boyfriend. Travis says
he wants to get back to his ranch roots, but Liz knows
Travis is running from something. Old feelings emerge
as they work together, but Liz can't help but wonder
if Travis is home to stay.

Reluctant Texas Rancher

Available March
wherever books are sold.

New York Times *and* USA TODAY *bestselling author*
Maya Banks presents book three in her miniseries
PREGNANCY & PASSION.

TEMPTED BY HER INNOCENT KISS

Available March 2012 from Harlequin Desire!

There came a time in a man's life when he knew he was well and truly caught. Devon Carter stared down at the diamond ring nestled in velvet and acknowledged that this was one such time. He snapped the lid closed and shoved the box into the breast pocket of his suit.

He had two choices. He could marry Ashley Copeland and fulfill his goal of merging his company with Copeland Hotels, thus creating the largest, most exclusive line of resorts in the world, or he could refuse and lose it all.

Put in that light, there wasn't much he could do except pop the question.

The doorman to his Manhattan high-rise apartment hurried to open the door as Devon strode toward the street. He took a deep breath before ducking into his car, and the driver pulled into traffic.

Tonight was the night. All of his careful wooing, the countless dinners, kisses that started brief and casual and became more breathless—all a lead-up to tonight. Tonight his seduction of Ashley Copeland would be complete, and then he'd ask her to marry him.

He shook his head as the absurdity of the situation hit him for the hundredth time. Personally, he thought William Copeland was crazy for forcing his daughter down Devon's throat.

Ashley was a sweet enough girl, but Devon had no desire

to marry anyone.

William had other plans. He'd told Devon that Ashley had no head for the family business. She was too softhearted, too naive. So he'd made Ashley part of the deal. The catch? Ashley wasn't to know of it. Which meant Devon was stuck playing stupid games.

Ashley was supposed to think this was a grand love match. She was a starry-eyed woman who preferred her animal-rescue foundation over board meetings, charts and financials for Copeland Hotels.

If she ever found out the truth, she wouldn't take it well.

And hell, he couldn't blame her.

But no matter the reason for his proposal, before the night was over, she'd have no doubts that she belonged to him.

What will happen when Devon marries Ashley?
Find out in Maya Banks's passionate new novel
TEMPTED BY HER INNOCENT KISS
Available March 2012 from Harlequin Desire!

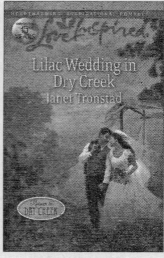

When Cat Barker ran away from the juvenile home she was raised in, she left more than an unstable childhood behind. She also left her first love, Jake Stone. Now, years later, Cat needs help, and there's only one person she can turn to—Jake, her daughter's secret father. Cat fears love and marriage but a daunting challenge renews her faith—and teaches them all a lesson about trust.

Lilac Wedding in Dry Creek
by Janet Tronstad

Harlequin *Presents*

USA TODAY bestselling author

Carol Marinelli

begins a daring duet.

THE SECRETS of XANOS

Two brothers alike in charisma and power; separated at birth and seeking revenge...

Nico has always felt like an outsider. He's turned his back on his parents' fortune to become one of Xanos's most powerful exports and nothing will stand in his way—until he stumbles upon a virgin bride....

Zander took his chances on the streets rather than spending another moment under his cruel father's roof. Now he is unrivaled in business—and the bedroom! He wants the best people around him, and Charlotte is the best PA! Can he tempt her over to the dark side...?

A SHAMEFUL CONSEQUENCE
Available in March

AN INDECENT PROPOSITION
Available in April